A SUSPENSE NOVEL

DON'T LOOK
BEHIND YOU

SAMUEL ROGERS

WILDSIDE PRESS

CHAPTER 1

*D*APHNE had never been more thankful to be anywhere than she was to find herself at last inside Dr. Macfarlane's gateway. She glanced over her shoulder down the little wooded road along which she had been hurrying. It was quite empty. She could see only the pink bars of sunlight across the hardbaked dirt, the weeds on either side, their leaves drooping and gray with dust, the unmoving foliage of the oak trees. She felt ashamed of her look, ashamed because it had taken such an effort to turn her head.

It reminded her of that winter years ago when the family had stayed at the farm until after Christmas, and almost every night she had been waked up by Tim mewing outside, downstairs on the front porch. She would wait then, hoping that Barbara or Jimmy would hear and go down to let him in; but she knew they would pretend to be asleep, because they could count on her softheartedness. She would get out of bed in the cold and feel her way downstairs, perfectly dark because there was no electricity, so that she could barely see the coat rack in the corner. She was sure something awful was behind it, but she would fumble for the bolt and chain, and open the door a few inches while Tim walked slowly in with his tail held high. Then she would draw the bolt, not bothering with the chain, and feel sure, absolutely sure, that the thing from behind the coat rack was after her.

At the foot of the stairs she would look around. It would be there, hidden among the shadows; but she would not allow herself to run. She would walk up, step by step, with Tim rubbing against her ankles as a faint consolation.

Well, this evening she had not run either, though she had certainly felt like it; but it didn't seem as if she could be hotter if she had run all the way. She wiped her face with her handkerchief, and the next moment caught herself listening. Not a sound! Then for the first time she realized that the air was full of the chirp of crickets—very faint, coming from all sides at once, like the heat vibrations made audible

3

or like a ringing in one's own head. They must have been chirping this way as she walked through the wood; she had never listened more intently but she had not noticed it. Of course that was because she had been listening for another kind of noise.

She put her handkerchief back into the little white kid purse that Harold had given her last week. Perhaps, after all, it was more ominous that the road remained empty. Whatever or whoever it was did not want to be seen. It could not be then just one of the other guests, as she had tried to persuade herself though if it had been his behavior was certainly odd. Well, she was safely here, and Harold would be walking home with her. At any ordinary time, she consoled herself, she would not have been nervous. It was just that now, with those scare headlines last week. . . . If only she had thought of them earlier! She hoped the subject would not come up tonight, but it probably would.

She turned again and started walking slowly up the gravel driveway. There must be several acres of gardens and lawns, and the house was much grander than she had expected. Dr. Macfarlane was so jolly and unpretentious that you did not think of him as being rich. Neat and white, with its tall columns in front, the house looked almost cool, if you could think of anything's ever looking cool again. There were three sprinklers playing on the lawn, which explained why it was so much greener than most of the lawns in town; though even here there were brownish patches, as if perhaps a circus had encamped here a few days ago. How delightful it would be, if she were in her bathing suit and could lie down on the grass under one of those sprinklers! The sun made little rainbows in the spray that drifted from them, like the rainbows around the prow of a ship. If she was not going to a party she would be tempted to wet her face and hands at any rate; but her white muslin dress that had been so fresh when she put it on was already beginning to look as droopy as the leaves of the nettles and bee balm beside the road. She could not risk getting it damp.

When she reached the porch she looked back again from the white columns. Beyond the lawn, under the pale evening sky, still a half hour before sunset, the woods stretched quiet and monotonous, not so much a landscape as an empty background. A night hawk dropped from high above them, caught itself with a faint "chug," and soared again. "He's trying to make them seem innocent and real, ' she thought, "but it doesn't fool me. They only look more treacherous."

She wheeled quickly as she heard the door opening behind her. "Did I scare you?" Dr. Macfarlane asked. "I saw you coming up the drive."

"Of course you didn't," she exclaimed, and felt that she was grinning from ear to ear in her relief at being no longer alone. She recalled how when she had first seen him at the hospital, during her nurse's aide training, she had thought his face looked coarse and sensual, and wondered how people could choose him for their doctor. Later she had come to think that he was one of the kindest and most understanding men she had ever known, and now as she smiled into his shiny face, with its large features rather crowded together, its tufted eyebrows, she could have flung her arms around him and kissed him. She had better not attempt it, though, because the poor man would certainly wonder why, and she could not bear to have to explain.

If she did not mention it she might forget it, forget the feeling at least. Perhaps after a cocktail she would no longer be able even to imagine that feeling, just as you forgot the peculiar lurking terror that never quite came to the surface in a bad dream—the kind of dream that did not develop into a nightmare but only prowled around and around you without coming nearer, like distant thunder threatening beneath the horizon.

"Where's your young man?" he asked. "I sort of counted on his driving you out. This is a hell of a night to walk."

"Harold?" she said. "He had to have two of his tires recapped. He won't get his car for several days."

"So he just left you flat, did he? I should think right now he'd have wanted to keep an eye on you. But I take it you have strong nerves."

She smiled at his compliment. If Dr. Macfarlane only knew!

But she must make it clear that poor Harold was not to blame. "He was calling for me at half-past six," she ex-

5

plained, "and when he didn't show up by seven I left a note and didn't wait any longer."

His small eyes stared at her from between their red lashes; his thick lips slowly smiled. "Naughty, naughty!" he said. "If you start punishing him now, what will it be later, once you've got him hog-tied?"

She laughed. "I guess he'll have to take his chance," she said. "As a matter of fact, the Psychology Department had a meeting this afternoon, but I thought it certainly should be over by six."

"My poor little Daphne," Dr. Macfarlane said, "department meetings are never over. That's one of the things you'll learn when you've married a professor."

They had stepped into the hall, and now he led her on into the huge living room. It had pale green walls and white woodwork, and there were bowls of lemon-colored marigolds on tables before the windows. Daphne could not make up her mind whether it was really much cooler than outside or only seemed so because it looked so airy and spacious. She was sure that Dr. Macfarlane had left the decorating of the house in the hands of his wife.

Daphne realized that this would be her first real party since she had come to Woodside over a year ago. If it had not been for Mother's illness she might have known more people, though of course until her engagement to Harold she had been just another student. From now on she would have to live up to her position as the fiancée of the most brilliant young psychologist on the faculty; and as she glanced around the room she could almost persuade herself that her recent scare in the woods had been a good thing: it made the people she would meet tonight seem relatively harmless, and she recalled how nervous she had been that she would not do Harold justice among his clever friends.

Two women had been standing together at the far end of the room, and now one of them came forward to greet her.

"Jeanne," Dr. Macfarlane said, "I don't think you've had the great pleasure of meeting Daphne Gray. Daphne and I are very good friends by now. I won't tell you how good, because I don't want to prejudice you against her. You've no idea what goes on at the hospital."

6

"It's unspeakable, I'm sure," Jeanne Macfarlane said, "but what I don't know won't hurt me."

She shook hands cordially with Daphne, and Daphne liked her at once. She was almost as homely as her husband but her face had the distinction his lacked: it reminded Daphne of a portrait by Frans Hals. Her mouse-colored hair was plastered back from her face; her white linen dress hung a little crooked.

"I'm going to call you Daphne," she said. "It would be absurd not to. And you must call me Jeanne."

"I've been trying to get her to call me Terry," Dr. Macfarlane exclaimed, "but it seems that she respects me even more than she loves me. However, closer acquaintance will remedy that. And now, Daphne, you must meet the real glamour girl of Woodside. Wanda, come over here with those panther steps of yours, and let this poor child have a look at you."

The other woman stayed where she was, but raised darkened eyelids and stared lazily at Daphne. Her short hair was olive-black, her face was oval and might have been beautiful if the flanges of her nose had not been so broad and thick. Daphne suspected that the paint on her lips had little relation to the real shape of her mouth.

"If you know him," she said to Daphne in a throaty voice, "I need explain no further."

"Her name," Dr. Macfarlane went on, "is Wanda Hatfield. Mrs. Paul Hatfield. Wouldn't you know she'd be named something like Wanda? Her man has deserted her too. Perhaps Harold and he will arrive together. And now if you girls will excuse me, I'll go make the cocktails."

"I feel quite jealous," Mrs. Hatfield said, sauntering now toward the middle of the room. "He wouldn't start them just for me. I try to make myself beautiful with a most expensive new lipstick. My dear, you couldn't imagine what it cost. It's supposed to be something super-super, though between you and me I don't believe you could tell the difference from a Woolworth product. And then my husband jumps out of the car after some bird or other, and my host won't mix me a drink."

"A bird?" Daphne asked. "You mean a real bird?"

7

This Mrs. Hatfield no doubt was pleasant and amusing, but Daphne was aware that she resented her: already she was trying to convince herself that the woman must be at least forty, while she knew quite well that she couldn't be over thirty-five.

"It was a real bird all right, but don't ask me what kind. Paul's the bird authority for the whole state, at least he thinks he is. When we were first married Paul tried to indoctrinate me, but I never got much beyond robins and crows. He's down in the college catalogue as a chemist, but his real passion is birds. I might add they're his only passion, as far as I've been able to discover." Her voice had grown even huskier, and Daphne realized with distaste that this was meant to be an allusion to her marital experience. "Don't think I object," Mrs. Hatfield went on, "if it suits the Chemistry Department."

Daphne smiled to herself at the thought of this Mrs. Hatfield on a bird walk, but her next question was eager.

"You mean he actually got out of the car to follow a bird he'd seen?"

"I certainly do. Except he didn't even see it, he just heard it. I didn't know any decent bird was around at this time of day. I left him a quarter of a mile back, prowling through the woods with his binoculars."

Daphne felt suddenly gay. This would explain it, surely: someone stalking a bird, trying not to be seen, to make no noise. It showed what reading the newspapers could do when you were tired. She must have been working too many hours at the hospital. She felt that she would have a lovely time tonight and could hardly wait for Harold to get here. Or was she quite as relieved as she liked to think?

She heard a man's laugh, abrupt and gay, and two men stepped into the room but neither one was Harold. The first one she knew fairly well: his name was Edwin Voigt; he was assistant professor of English and played the piano beautifully. She had heard him at one or two of the Sunday afternoon concerts. He was a slender neat man, negatively handsome, with a brown curly mustache which stood out assertively, as if to protest against the vagueness of his other features.

8

The second, the man who had laughed, was a good deal younger, younger even than Harold: he must be in his early twenties. He was so dark that he looked Spanish or South American, so handsome in a cardboard sort of way that she could picture him glancing over heaps of fan mail. He moved, he stood, with an easy grace which she longed maliciously to think was theatrical.

"Edwin," Jeanne Macfarlane said, after she had greeted them, "I think you know Daphne Gray but I'm sure Dave doesn't. Perhaps I should explain, Daphne, that Dave is the rising star of our Biology Department. He has a wonderful way with mice. He was thrilled to be asked tonight, because he said he'd seen you several times on the street and wondered who you were."

The young man gave her a glance both dark and bright. "That's not all I said," he exclaimed in a pleasant voice far less abrupt than his laugh. "My name, by the way, is Dave Fulton." Daphne was relieved at any rate that this striking young man was not Mr. Hatfield.

"It's evidently not my night," Wanda said to her, although she was looking at Dave. "You notice that he didn't even glance at *me*." And Daphne had an idea that she was not speaking entirely in fun.

Edwin Voigt came over to talk to her, and she tried as she always did to forget his mustache and decide what he actually looked like. His face was sensitive, with nice brows and cheekbones, but strangely lacking in luster. She wondered if anything she could say would make it really come to life: it would be sort of a game to try. But just then Dr. Macfarlane returned with the cocktails, and she was taking her first sip when Harold stepped through the doorway.

His yellow hair was rumpled. He glanced around the room with his large and rather startled blue eyes, eyes that had the incalculability, the charm, she had always thought, of some animal not really used to people. Then the instant he saw her, his whole face lighted and changed, and for the moment she forgot everyone else in the room.

"Well!" he exclaimed. "You ought to be ashamed of yourself. Hullo, Jeanne. Hullo, Terry. That girl over there deserves a good spanking."

9

Daphne could see that his joking manner covered a very real relief. It made her feel guilty, but at the same time it comforted her for it seemed to suggest that after all she had had a right to be scared.

"Go ahead," Wanda exclaimed. "Don't let us cramp your style!"

Harold wiped his forehead: he looked dusty and terribly hot.

"I've been peering under every bush and behind every tree," he went on. "I didn't know what I might find. I wouldn't have cared so much if you hadn't left that note and told me you were taking the little road through the woods."

Daphne held her breath for a moment: would anyone bring it up? But no, Dr. Macfarlane had begun to tell a joke as he handed Harold his cocktail. The danger was past.

A thickset middle-aged man appeared in the doorway. Though she could not possibly have heard him above the general chatter, he gave her the impression of moving with exceptional quietness. His face might have been carved very sharply, very neatly, out of wood; his eyes moved perkily; his head was cocked like a bird's.

"Hi, Paul!" Dr. Macfarlane shouted. "You're just in time. Daphne, this is Paul Hatfield, another one of those damn professors, but you might as well get used to them."

"How do you do, Miss Gray?" Professor Hatfield said. His voice was soft and very precise. "Harold Forster has told me about you. I hoped I'd be meeting you one of these days."

Daphne felt that she must not let him get away from her. She walked beside him as he moved toward the table where Jeanne was pouring him a drink.

"I think we almost met earlier this evening," she said.

"Really? How was that? I'm sorry we didn't." His voice had a kind of old-fashioned politeness that made her decide he could not be so young as she had thought at first.

"Mrs. Hatfield told us that you were chasing a bird through the woods."

He cocked his head. "Well, yes, I suppose you could describe it that way. As a matter of fact, it was nothing in the

10

least spectacular." He lowered his voice with a flattering effect of intimacy. "It was just an ordinary wood thrush, but there are not so many around here, and I happen to be very fond of them."

"I thought I heard someone—or something—in the woods as I came out here, and I'm sure it must have been you."

"Do you think so?" He looked vague and dubious. "May I ask which way you came?"

"Along that little road through the woods that ends just opposite the gate."

Through the window and across the lawn she could see the white gateposts and the line of trees behind them. The woods were dark now, almost gray, beneath the flushed and cloudless sky. They seemed miles away from this room; they might be anywhere in the world.

"Ah, then it couldn't have been I," he said. "We came by the main highway. My thrush was in that bit of woodland over there behind you, just next to the cemetery."

Daphne frowned at herself, because her burst of gaiety had gone; because those woods were once more something treacherous and strange—within whose dry gray shadows anything might be lurking, might be silently, hungrily waiting.

She was thankful for the second cocktail which Dr. Macfarlane was pouring into her glass.

CHAPTER II

*W*ELL, I don't suppose there's been any more news about our local murderer?"

It was Professor Hatfield who asked the question. His ingratiating tone would have made Daphne think, if she had not caught his words, that he was inquiring in a kindly way about someone's victory garden. Dinner was half over, and the talk until now had been mostly speculation about the Sicilian campaign. Daphne was surprised that she did not mind this allusion to the crime. She felt even a little curious, as if in some remote way, after her experience in the woods, she were personally involved. Of course this

11

rather exciting feeling was the result of the cocktails, and the delicious red wine with which the waitress was always filling up her glass.

She looked at Harold now, on her right, and could see that he was pleased the subject of the murder had come up. He would not have dared introduce it himself, of course, because he knew how she hated to talk of such things.

She gave him her warmest smile, to show him that she did not mind what they talked about, that she could hold her own with anyone; and she felt that her eyes must be very bright, her cheeks glowing through their tan. A prejudiced person like Harold might even think for the moment that she was beautiful.

"I haven't heard of anything," he said. "If they had found the body sooner it would have been much easier going. I think they calculated it must have been lying in that thicket for at least two weeks. How about it, Terry? You saw the girl, didn't you?"

"Sure. I just dropped in for fun with some of the boys. It would be hard to tell exactly how long she was out there, but she'd certainly been there for some time. There was no doubt of that."

"Two weeks!" Wanda exclaimed. "I didn't realize it was so long."

Across the table, between Edwin Voigt and Dave Fulton, she had been carrying on, to Daphne's amusement, a half-whispered conversation, glancing from beneath her sticky lashes first at one and then the other of these two good-looking young men; but concentrating certainly on Dave.

"You mean to say she was lying for two weeks right here in these woods where anybody might have stumbled over her? But I should think in this heat. . . ."

For an instant Daphne sickeningly recalled the dead horse she and Barbara had come upon at the edge of the swamp near the ledges: that awful smell which had penetrated dizzily to the very center of their heads as the breeze shifted, the caked dust, the unbelievable flies. She must not think of that while food was before her.

"My dear, if you had listened to me I could have told you all about it," Mr. Hatfield said gently. "I've been following the case with great interest, what little there is to follow. It was precisely on account of the heat . . ."

"Really, Paul!" Jeanne Macfarlane exclaimed. "There are limits! Remember poor Daphne isn't used to our dinner table autopsies." She flashed at Daphne her direct kindly smile. "When Paul and Terry get together," she said, "they sometimes are positively ghoulish. Wanda and I became hardened to it long ago, and I think they simply love getting a fresh and comparatively innocent listener, like you or Edwin, for example, whom they can shock."

Daphne glanced at Edwin Voigt and caught his dim eye for an instant: she guessed that he was not enjoying the conversation any more than she was, and it gave her a sense of fellow feeling. Edwin made a slight face, as if he had tasted something unpleasant.

"Thanks at any rate for the 'innocent'," he said.

"Daphne's all right," Terry protested. (She could think of him now quite easily as Terry; that too was because of the cocktails.) "What the hell! She's a nurse's aide. She's worked in the men's surgical ward. She ought to be able to stand anything."

That was quite true, Daphne admitted to herself: if she could only think of this business in a matter-of-fact way, as she was beginning, just beginning, to think of her work at the hospital!

"Oh it's all right with me," she said. "Harold simply loves horrors too. It's one of the first things I discovered about him. I'm trying to break him of the habit."

Dave Fulton looked at her, smiling to show teeth that might have advertised a dental cream. "*I* don't like horrors," he told her; and he managed to give her the impression that he had brushed all the others aside, including poor Wanda. "I think you and I have probably a lot in common."

She felt Harold's hand on her arm. "Darling," he said, "you talk as if you didn't realize that what may seem horrible to you, may not seem horrible at all to a doctor, or a psychologist, or a criminologist. It may merely seem interesting—and sometimes it may be completely fascinating."

"Of course I realize it," she said. "Don't look so solemn, darling."

13

Why, for example, should she remember that horse with such loathing when she had dissected a cat quite calmly, at least after the first day, in Boilogy 2? It was a ten-year-old-boy picking blackberries who had discovered this girl's body. Supposing that Barbara and herself, that hot afternoon by the ledges, had found not the body of a horse. . . . She could not bear to think of it. She finished the wine in her glass.

"Personally I don't believe they'll ever get him," Terry said. "They haven't a single damn thing to go on."

"Not this time," Harold agreed. "But perhaps the next time there *will* be something—especially if they find the body sooner."

"The next time!" Dave spoke crisply. "What makes you think there will be a next time?"

"He doesn't," Jeanne said. "You're just trying to scare us, aren't you, Harold?"

She looked straight at him, and as Daphne watched her homely face, so kind, so really intelligent, she tried to smile at her, as she had done just now at Harold, to prove that she did not need protection.

"Ah!" Professor Hatfield exclaimed, and she could imagine him raising his finger to make his point. "If this girl was killed by a sadistic maniac, as seems almost certain, there is at least a fair probability that the cirme will be repeated."

Edwin Voigt had been tugging at his mustache. "What makes you think it's a homicidal maniac?" he asked rather testily. "It seems to me you scientists get the most romantic ideas. Why couldn't it be just a tramp, or a drunken soldier perhaps? Why couldn't it be robbery, or good old-fashioned rape? The girl started to scream. He lost his head and tried to make her shut up."

"In that case," Professor Hatfield said, as if he were speaking with the greatest tact to a rather slow student, "he would hardly have been apt to draw a knife. He'd have been much more likely to knock her over the head, or even strangle her."

"He was a sadist all right," Terry said heartily. "Boy, if you'd seen the body! Why, to begin with . . ."

"Terry!" Jeanne's voice was sharp and yet not in the least cross. Daphne could not imagine her ever losing her temper.

"Okay, okay. I was only going to say . . ."

"Terry darling, you can tell *me* afterwards," Wanda interrupted. "At least you can give me an idea. I'd be really curious. A girl friend of mine once spent a week end with a man in Chicago. It wasn't what it sounds like. I mean it was quite innocent as far as she was concerned. At least that's what she said. I mean it was a house party. He must have been an awful old degenerate, though, because she said he had a couple of books about tortures and so on bound in human skin."

"I doubt it very much," Paul Hatfield said. "I've always doubted it. He probably bought them for some fancy price as curiosa, but I doubt very much whether human skin could ever make a durable binding."

"But even granting our man was crazy," Edwin insisted, "I don't see why he might not have been just passing through. He needn't be a local product, need he?"

"Not necessarily," Harold said, "but I'm rather inclined to think so."

His face was concentrated and very much alive; his eyes were gleaming. He shook a couple of strands of damp light hair back from his forehead. This was just the kind of discussion he loved, and although she disliked it so much herself, Daphne could forgive him because when he was really interested in anything he became so handsome.

"Landru roved about a little," he went on, "but he stayed pretty near the suburbs of Paris. His case is rather different, though: it seems to have been largely a business affair, though I've no doubt he enjoyed it. But Jack the Ripper, now, to take a classic example. That fellow stuck to one section of London where presumably he lived. And Fritz Haarmann . . ."

"Who's he?" Dave asked. "I never heard of him."

His tone annoyed Daphne, because it seemed to imply that no such person existed.

"You don't know about Fritz Haarmann?" Professor Hatfield asked with the gentlest air of reproof. "He was a

15

butcher who lived in Hanover just after the World War. It's thought he murdered something like forty young men. He didn't remember exactly. I suppose for sheer gruesomeness . . ."

"That will do, Paul," Jeanne said. "I seem to have developed into the official censor for the evening, but it's quite evident we need one."

"But if the town of Woodside is harboring a local Jack the Ripper," Edwin Voigt said with a touch of sarcasm, "I don't see why he waited until now."

"That's downright silly!" Wanda exclaimed. "You know it is, Edwin. There always has to be a first time, even for much more innocent things than murder. And it's always *le premier pas qui coûte*. At least that's what the French say, and they have a reputation for being pretty knowledgeable."

"Well, if you have to begin sometime," Edwin said, "you also have to end sometime, and I don't see why this might not be the last time as well as the first. Jack the Ripper was never caught, but he stopped eventually."

"Eventually—yes," Professor Hatfield said with a faint but ominous stress on the word.

"Come, come now," Jeanne exclaimed, "you can't make me believe that a college town like Woodside, miles from anywhere, would be likely to harbor a real honest-to-God mass murderer."

"On the contrary," Harold said, and from the eager stress of his tone Daphne was sure that he would overstate his point, as he was apt to do in the exhilaration of an argument, "I'm surprised that there are no records, at least so far as I know, of such a murderer in a college community. I should think it would be an ideal place for one. You have a lot of high-strung individuals, numbers of them more or less frustrated. They're curious; they're often restless. They're certainly far better read than factory workers, say, or even businessmen. They're far more apt to be up on the literature of murder, from Agamemnon and Macbeth down, and everyone knows the enormous power of suggestion on a slightly unbalanced mind. Jean-Baptiste Troppmann, the Alsatian, who murdered a whole family in a particularly

16

brutal way, seems to have got the idea from *The Wandering Jew* which he was always rereading. Gilles de Rais was artistic and scholarly, as well as being a fine soldier, and yet he tortured to death heaven knows how many boys—well over a hundred. He admitted, if I remember correctly, that he'd been influenced by reading Suetonius. The Marquis de Sade was an intelligent fellow, and incidentally a very discerning psychologist. . . ."

"I don't claim to be a psychologist," Paul Hatfield remarked, "but aren't you a bit overemphasizing one side of the question? After all, weren't the Maréchal de Rais and the Marquis de Sade rather exceptional? And of course the Marquis de Sade never actually committed murder, so far as I know. Haarmann was shrewd, yes. So was Landru. So was Smith—he was the man who drowned his wives in a bathtub," he explained politely to Daphne, "but they none of them were what you would call cultivated; they were none of them intellectuals. I can't really imagine any of them on our faculty, can you?"

"And how about Jack the Ripper?" Dave asked. "I suppose he was a cultured fellow with an Oxford accent."

"He may have been," Harold replied calmly. "For all we know, he may have written polite essays or painted Pre-Raphaelite pictures. As a matter of fact, we're dealing with a very special kind of madman. It doesn't seem to me even that it's quite accurate to describe him that way. Apart from his compulsion, which only seizes him periodically, he may be quite sane . . . or at least he may appear so. Our own local man, because in spite of Edwin I still think he belongs around here, why he might be anyone at all. He doesn't have to have flopping ears or buck teeth. He might be both interesting and attractive. He might be one of us here to-night."

Daphne glanced up at him quickly: a drop of sweat hung from the end of his nose; his face was tense and eager. Of course he was saying really more than he meant but he was not joking.

The gaiety, the confidence, that the cocktails and the wine had given her left her suddenly; she felt only a little confused, a little sick. She made a desperate attempt to

17

clear her mind, so that she could consider objectively what Harold had said. If she could only see it in proportion, as Harold had meant it, she would be able to laugh at it. Anyone here might be that murderer, just as anyone here might have contracted leprosy, and the one case was just about as probable as the other: that was all Harold meant. She could see it that way but she could not feel it.

The wine which had been her friend was now her enemy. She looked around the large candlelighted table which seemed to be floating like an island in the middle of the dim white-walled room. She looked, she hardly dared to look, from face to face. If it would have been horrible to meet some strange madman in that hot gray wood, someone crouching behind a thicket of half-wilted blackberry bushes, how much more horrible to meet someone familiar, some friend, who would suddenly turn into the awful thing you couldn't imagine. Once when she was a little girl she had dreamed she was alone in a big dark house. Suddenly Mother had appeared, and she ran to her with open arms, delighted to escape from the kind of bumbling darkness. But Mother's eyes were not her own. They looked like grapes or red transparent marbles: it wasn't Mother at all. and Daphne had screamed and struggled in her sleep. It would be like that.

Then all at once, in the momentary silence, she heard again through the large screened windows open to the lawn the incessant chirping of the crickets; the air was just as full of it in here as it was outside. It seemed to be hinting that nothing—no walls, no lights—could be any protection.

"Now really," Wanda began, and Daphne felt that she must at least pretend to be listening: this qualm of hers would pass—"now really, you don't mean that one of us girls could have done that job?"

Harold smiled faintly. "Well, I admit I wasn't thinking of you. That would be highly improbable. Not impossible, I suppose, but there's every chance that it's a man."

"I guess I'd be the most likely suspect," Terry exclaimed. "I'm used to carving up people. I do it every day."

"For that very reason you'd be the least likely," Harold said. "You couldn't be a successful surgeon if you were not

18

calm at the sight of blood. It can't be any treat to you."

"You don't know me!" Terry rolled his eyes and gritted his teeth. "It may be just super-self-control, and of course this may have been my first. As Wanda says, there always has to be a beginning. Besides, isn't the least likely always the guilty one in the end?"

"Not any longer," Paul Hatfield explained. "The one that's obviously least likely has become the most likely, if you see what I mean; and so he genuinely is the least likely. Fifteen or twenty years ago you always had to be suspicious of a bedridden and paralyzed old grandmother, particularly if the crime was one involving exceptional agility. But now you can be virtually sure the poor old soul is innocent, just because the naïve reader has been trained to believe she is guilty."

"Nowadays I'd be the guilty one," Edwin said with a dry unamused chuckle. "The quiet little man that no one especially suspects because they keep forgetting he exists."

"Not at all," Professor Hatfield said courteously. "The artistic temperament is always under suspicion." He glanced sharply at Edwin. "And so it ought to be," he added, as if he were paying him a special compliment.

"I don't really like mystery stories," Daphne said: she had not opened her mouth for she didn't know how long, and felt that she must say something. "They always seem to have elaborate timetables and train connections that are very important to keep straight, and I never can; and if they don't get me all confused, they generally scare me to death."

"Of course," Paul Hatfield stated, "it's a bad thing to have the murders in a straight detective story committed by a madman, because as Harold said just now it might be almost anyone. You don't have to worry about motive, and the whole thing is quite arbitrary."

"I don't know that I agree with you," Harold said. "In real life, of course, it's not arbitrary at all. When I said any one of us might have committed this particular murder, it wouldn't be actually unrelated to the context of his apparently normal character, or even of his daily life. It would only seem so. And it would by no means be hit or miss. The

19

fact that Jack the Ripper wasn't caught in spite of his striking again and again in very much the same locality, where everyone was on the lookout for him, would certainly seem to prove that he planned carefully. It would take imagination, of course, to get some insight into the peculiar nature of his planning, to catch his tempo, as it were, his psychological color or atmosphere. If I were a detective in a case like this, supposing it continues developing, I think the first thing I'd try to do would be to put myself as nearly as possible in the murderer's place, to pretend I was he, to feel my way into his mind. It's an old gag, but it's sound common sense nonetheless."

"I should think that might sometimes work in the case of a sane criminal," Jeanne said, "but when the man is crazy . . ."

"My dear Jeanne, I'm always trying to din into people the fact that there is no hard-and-fast boundary line between the sane and the insane. And that is especially true in a case like this. There is no real difference in kind, one might say, between the most innocent and natural behavior and a series of the most brutal murders: it's rather a difference of emphasis, of degree. The criminal violence involved is not something utterly new and strange: it's just the gross, the pathological distortion of something normal, something already there, in all of us. Most of the time we move along complacently, and take our sanity for granted. But haven't you sometimes felt, when you've been sick or tired or worried, that sanity was like a tightrope strung across a great gulf, that you have to walk over it and if the slightest little adjustment should go wrong you'd topple off and never stop falling . . . that if you let yourself even look down you might grow dizzy and have the devil of a time keeping your balance? You're mighty lucky if you haven't."

"I've never thought of it in just that way," Jeanne said reflectively, "but yes, I see what you mean."

"I suppose," Professor Hatfield remarked with a ruminating air, as if he had scarcely been listening for the last few minutes, "there is every chance that the next victim, if there should be another, would be a young girl—just as the first one was."

20

CHAPTER III

*L*OOKING in the window from the porch, Daphne could
see Edwin's face as he played. Music was what brought
it to life, she could see that now; she had never been near
enough at the public concerts. It was as if a soft lamplight
had been kindled in the depths of his pupils; his whole face
was composed and tranquil, and no longer a mere dim background for his mustache.

She could understand why music was sometimes helpful
in nervous cases. Edwin was playing some French harpsichord pieces from the seventeenth century, pavans, cou-
rantes, and sarabands. They were at once frail and spirited,
full of a distant life, and yet so peaceful that they brought
tears to her eyes. Her scary walk, the conversation at dinner, seemed far away and quite unimportant: they were like
the dust that clung to your clothes, that got rubbed into
your skin, on such a day as this, but that suddenly was all
washed off when you plunged into still deep water.

The music stopped and she turned regretfully away. The
darkness of the long porch was cut at intervals by the light
streaming from the windows, and here and there glowed the
sparks of cigarettes. There were fireflies flashing over the
lawn; most of them were close to the ground, though now
and then one would appear, surprisingly, among the con-
stellations like a bright momentary star. There was still no
breath of wind.

Daphne sat down in one of the comfortable wicker chairs;
she chose one not too near the rest of the people, because
she would much rather not have to talk for a few minutes,
unless it was with Harold, and he was busy with Professor
Hatfield at the far end of the porch. But the next moment
Dave Fulton, with a tall drink in his hand, came and sat
down in the chair next to hers.

"Would you like one of these?" he asked. "Wouldn't you
like this one? I haven't touched it."

"No, thanks," she replied rather shortly. It had seemed

21

to her that his manner toward Harold at dinner had been heckling, and she was sure that quietly, within himself, he must be conceited.

"You better take it," he urged. "It will cool you off wonderfully."

His insistence annoyed her. "I told you I didn't want it," she said snappishly.

He chuckled with the abruptness she had noticed before and which was such a contrast to his smooth speaking voice. "I can see now that you wouldn't take one if you were dying of thirst. You don't like me, do you? Why's that?"

"I don't know you well enough to either like or dislike you," she said.

"Whew!" he exclaimed. "I don't need ice in my drink after that! Go ahead, take it! Or how about our sharing it?"

"I wish you wouldn't keep bothering me with that old whisky," she said, almost with tears in her voice. "I was just trying to think of that lovely music. I wanted to get a little quiet, so I could really remember it. And now I've forgotten it already."

"Oh I *am* sorry," he said. "I've been awfully clumsy, haven't I?"

She did not answer, and for a minute neither spoke. Daphne stared at the moving pattern of the fireflies and tried in vain to recapture the feeling of peace that he had disturbed. She felt hot and sulky, and also a little foolish. A car passed along the highroad, a hundred yards away, beyond the hedge, and she could imagine, in the lifeless air, that she could smell from here the hot greasy smoke of its exhaust. The clink of the ice in Dave's glass made her suddenly very thirsty. She even wondered if he were shaking it on purpose, just to torment her. Then from the invisible woods beyond the gateway, cutting through the steady chirping that you only heard when you listened, there came a penetrating throaty whistle.

Daphne jumped, and barely stopped herself from crying out. "Good heavens!" she exclaimed. "What was that?"

"Did it startle you?" he asked. "It's only a tree toad.

22

They're very small but they make a surprising amount of noise. Have you ever seen one? They're really charming."

She would not have expected him to recognize the charm of tree toads, although Jeanne had told her that he was a biologist.

"I just love them," she said, "but I hardly ever run across them. I love all kinds of toads."

"Even the great big ones that hop around gardens?"

"Of course. Why not? I adore their faces, and I love the smooth feel of their stomachs."

"Good for you!" he exclaimed. "I'll carve you one sometime. That is if you'd like one."

"Are you a sculptor," she asked, "as well as a biologist?"

"Hardly that," he said, "but I love to whittle, especially animals. I quite approve of your liking toads. So many people are conditioned against them."

A few minutes ago, she realized, she would have considered his tone patronizing; but now she did not mind, because he seemed so evidently to mean what he said. She admitted too, in common justice, that listening to him here in the dark where she could not see his rather theatrical appearance he did not sound theatrical at all.

"Do you know," he went on presently, "it's quite true what Jeanne was telling you."

"What is that?" she asked. "I don't remember."

"That I was thrilled you were coming here tonight. I'd seen you several times lately on the street or walking through the campus, and I wondered who you were."

"If you didn't know," she asked skeptically, "how did you know it was I you were going to meet tonight?"

"Ah, I found out. In fact I must admit that I followed you the last time."

"You followed me," she said with only a halfhearted attempt to sound indignant. "I don't think that was very nice."

"Oh, I kept at a discreet distance. No one would have guessed I was on your track, and you see you had no idea of it yourself. I followed you to the hospital and I saw you talking to Terry in the lobby. You were in uniform, so I had a hunch that was where you were going. And then, shall I confess everything?"

23

"You might as well," Daphne said, "after you've gone this far."

"When Terry told me who you were, I brazenly up and asked him to invite me out here sometime when you were coming."

Daphne could not help smiling and was glad he could not see her face. She loved people to like her; she loved to be praised; she knew it quite well and did not even pretend to be ashamed of it. "If I were beautiful and charming, like Barbara," she had sometimes thought, "there might be the risk of my growing vain; but since there's no danger of that, I might as well enjoy what attention comes my way."

"Did he tell you I was engaged to Harold?" she asked.

"That was the first thing he did tell me. Sort of a jolt, wasn't it? But after all, you might have been married. And I suppose you do sometimes see other men . . . or is Harold the jealous type?"

"Not at all," she said. "I see whoever I want to. So does Harold."

"You know the thing that puzzles me," he went on, "is that I'd never run across you before. After all, Woodside's not New York. It's not even Milwaukee."

"This is only the second year I've been here," she explained.

"That accounts for it then. Last winter I was at Columbia on a fellowship, damn it! Did your family move here or did you come here for college?"

"I came with Mother," she said. "She was ill, and everyone told us that Dr. Pearson was the best man for her. We took an apartment, and I finished my undergraduate work here in February."

"Will you let me meet her sometime?" Dave asked.

"She died this April," Daphne said. "She had been very wretched during the last months."

He did not speak for a minute. Then he said: "Clumsy again, aren't I?"

"Not this time," Daphne said. "How could you possibly have guessed?"

"And now you're alone?"

"Yes. I kept the apartment. I'd grown fond of it."

24

"You have no other family?"

"I have a married sister in Quantico, where her husband is in training; and of course there's Jimmy, but he's in the South Pacific. Jimmy's my brother. He's two years older than I am." She was surprised that she had given him these details.

"But didn't you take a roommate?"

"No," Daphne said. "I don't mind being alone. At least I don't think I'd want anyone else there. After Mother, I mean."

"But aren't you awfully lonely?"

"I might have been lonely if it hadn't been for Harold."

"Lucky Harold!" Dave exclaimed.

"Daphne," a voice broke in, "won't you have a whisky and soda?" Edwin Voigt stood in front of her, with a glass in each hand.

"I'd love one," she said, and reached gratefully for the tall glass.

"You wouldn't take one when I offered it to you," Dave said reproachfully.

"I wasn't thirsty then. Besides you hadn't been playing such beautiful music. How could I refuse anything from Edwin?"

Just then Wanda walked up to them and sat down in the chair on the other side of Dave.

"There's something about him, isn't there?" she said to Daphne. "I see you've discovered it already. We women flock around him like flies."

"Come on, Wanda!" Dave said, and Daphne was amused to see that he was really embarrassed. "Where do you get that stuff?"

"That's really part of his charm," Wanda explained. "He's so unconscious of it. Whenever a new girl comes along I'm always curious to watch her fall. But you still love Wanda just the same, don't you, darling?"

She reached over and took his hand. He drew it away with his brusque laugh; but Daphne wondered what he would have done if she had not been there.

"Come along, Edwin?" she said. "I'm afraid we're not wanted."

"You certainly are!" Dave exclaimed; but Daphne had already risen, and was walking with Edwin toward the dark end of the porch.

"I simply loved your music," she said. "I'd never heard anything quite like it."

"It really should be played on the harpsichord." Edwin's voice sounded exceptionally colorless after Dave's. "Chambonnières was the leading harpsichord player at the court of Louis XIV, at least during the early part of his reign."

Daphne had learned that he made a point of never talking emotionally about music, never showing the least enthusiasm. When he spoke of it at all, it was in the most dryly factual way which was apt to make one's own praise sound insincere.

The tree toad whistled again, and now that Daphne knew what it was she liked the sound. For the first time since dinner she could see the outline of the woods: above them the sky was turning silvery, and the stars had grown small and faint. Suddenly she recalled something she had said a few minutes ago to Dave: "I don't mind being alone." It always had been true, certainly, until tonight; but now she dreaded the thought of the close empty apartment. "If only Mother were still there," she thought, "if Mother were there sick, in her great bed by the window, I'd be as brave as a lion."

But to hear Harold's footsteps going down the stairs, fainter and fainter, like noises when you fell asleep, to imagine that someone else, perhaps, was eagerly listening for that sound. . . .

"Darling!" It was Harold's voice. He had come quietly up behind her. "I think it's time for us to be going, don't you? The Hatfields offered us a lift, but I said I thought we'd rather walk. How about it? Of course it is hot, but it's not much more than a mile through the woods, and the moon is just rising."

Daphne turned to him quickly. How thankful she was that she had Harold! She wondered at this moment, as she did quite often, just why she could not bring herself to marry him right away. Perhaps it was because she still could not help being a little afraid of him sometimes, especially in company; and also of course because she had not yet got over the shock of Mother's death. It was delightful learning to know him gradually, to feel that there was no hurry; and certainly, with Harold, there was no excuse for ever feeling lonely again.

"I'd love to walk," she said, "if you'll promise to protect me."

CHAPTER IV

*A*S THEY passed through the gateway into the road, Harold put his arm around Daphne. It was too hot to walk that way for long, but it was comforting to feel her firm young body close beside him, to know that she was really there, that she was really his, that he could always count upon her.

He had not found the evening very satisfactory. To begin with, he had drunk too much, at first because he had been worried at her leaving without him, and then, having got such a start with the cocktails, he had continued drinking pretty steadily. He felt no longer any exhilaration, merely a sultry heaviness through his mind and body, and he was sure that tomorrow he would be good for nothing. And because of the alcohol he had also talked too much. He had held forth noisily at the dinner table, and afterwards on the porch to Paul and Jeanne.

He stopped now a few yards down the little road, and took his arm from around Daphne's waist to remove his necktie and open his shirt collar. Though the moon was still hidden by the trees the wood was no longer a dense black mass: a dingy gloaming filled the open spaces, like the remote reflection of a forest fire, but you could not yet make out the pattern of the tree trunks or tell what was near and what was far away. The harsh chirp of insects drilled into his head, rising, subsiding, rising, in a rhythm that suggested the waves on a beach. He wondered if that rhythm really existed or if it were just an illusion of his own hearing.

"Whew!" he exclaimed. "These certainly are the dog days!"

27

"Why are they called that?" she asked. "I've sometimes wondered."

"I believe it's because Procyon, the little Dog Star, rises at this time of year just before the sun. The Greeks invented the term, or perhaps it was even the Babylonians. But popularly they are supposed to be the days when the heat drives dogs mad."

"It's a little better now than it was," she said. "I wouldn't mind it so much if there wasn't that perpetual smell of dust."

He pulled her arm through his and they walked on again very slowly.

"You gave me quite a start when I found you had left without me," he said. "Why did you do it?"

"I suppose I was just cross, in a bad mood," she confessed. "It must have been the heat. I was in the children's orthopedic ward this afternoon, way up under the roof, and I thought I'd suffocate. I pity those poor little children. But I did give you a half hour's leeway. Don't you think that was pretty generous?"

"Of course the meeting dragged on and on, and needless to say nothing was accomplished. Not a damn thing. And then I had to take a shower and I had to shave."

"It didn't make any difference. Everyone else was late."

"Nothing ever begins on time at the Macfarlanes'. You can always count on that. I should have told you."

"You couldn't have paid me to start out alone," she said after a minute, "if I'd known you had such horrible ideas about the murder. I mean about there perhaps being others . . . and the murderer just lurking anywhere. The newspaper account must have been at least a week ago, wasn't it? And it said the actual crime took place long before that. I certainly thought the whole affair was over and done with, just as Edwin said. To tell the truth, I didn't give it a thought until I got into these woods: I was too annoyed with you. But why didn't you warn me, darling?"

"Well, of course you *did* promise to wait for me. But seriously, I knew how you hate to talk about such things. I don't wonder, because you belong to such a completely different world. And then, to be quite frank, I think Edwin's probably right. Most of the time tonight I was just shooting off my jaw to hear myself talk."

"I did think you were exaggerating a little," she admitted. "Sometimes it's hard to tell how much you really do mean."

"When Terry and Paul Hatfield and I get together," he said, "it's pretty safe to discount three quarters of what you hear. That goes for all of us."

"The Hatfields are a funny couple!" she exclaimed. "I like him much better than I do her. Tell me about them."

"There's not much to tell. My suspicion is that he's her husband in name only, and has been for a good many years. But he seems to take it philosophically. He's really a most distinguished chemist, you know. He's doing some secret experiments with war gas, working twelve hours a day. Wanda's just the way she seems, only not so much so."

"She could hardly be that," Daphne said.

"You may have noticed that just now she's crazy about Dave."

Abruptly, from close by, a whippoorwill started calling; it must have called a dozen times. In the dry unmoving air the sound had no atmosphere: it might have been made inside a room, by some harsh throaty wood-wind. For an instant after it stopped the night rang with stillness.

"You jumped," he said accusingly. "Good Lord, I hope all that foolish talk didn't really upset you!"

"No," she said. "It wasn't the talk. At least it wouldn't have, I think. But Harold, I was going to tell you . . . as soon as I could bear to . . ."

"Yes?" he said, and pressed her arm encouragingly.

"I'm sure that something—or someone—was following me when I walked along here this evening. At least it wasn't following me exactly. It was moving along beside me through the woods, to the right, along there, where the undergrowth is so thick. It began fairly soon after I'd passed the cemetery and got well into the woods. I took this road because you said it was a short cut and I thought it would be prettier. At first I thought I imagined it. I'd stop and it would stop. Then when I started on, it would go on. But sometimes it wouldn't stop quite so soon as I did. It was like that game of twenty steps: when the person that's 'it' turns suddenly around, and if he sees anyone moving, that one has to go back to the starting point. But whatever this was, it didn't go back, it always kept on. Of course sometimes I wouldn't hear it, and I'd try to pretend that it was gone. But then I'd hear it suddenly closer than ever, and I'm sure once or twice I even saw the bushes moving. It was stealthy and horrid. That's when I remembered the murder, and after that I didn't dare stop. I just walked faster and faster."

"You poor little thing!" he exclaimed. "I don't wonder. I would have myself. And then to have us rub your face in it all through dinner! I'm sure, though, it really wasn't anything bad. It may have been some animal, or a child looking for berries, if any have survived this drought. Or it may have been some mischievous boy deliberately trying to scare you. I remember how we used to love sneaking on people when I was a kid, and if we could really startle them it was a grand success. I can see just how you felt, though. You wondered what it was; then you thought of the murderer. Naturally enough that was somewhat chilling. The very fact of your fear made you convinced that there must be a reason for it, and then of course things went from bad to worse. It's a strange thing how you can work yourself up to the verge of panic through sheer autosuggestion."

Even as he talked he wondered whether he himself were wholly convinced. Speaking of suggestion, he was interested to observe that he at any rate took her story more seriously than he would have done before tonight's discussion. In spite of himself, a chill went up his spine at the bare idea, no matter how far-fetched, of the murderer prowling around Daphne. Yet somehow it did not surprise him.

He released her arm, and put his own once more about her waist.

"Of course I kept telling myself that I was foolish," she said. "But I must say it didn't do much good—at least not at the time."

"I think you got just what was coming to you," he said tenderly, "and if it will keep you from wandering alone into the country, for the next week or so, it was probably a good thing."

"No danger of that!" she exclaimed. "You couldn't drag me beyond the last street lamp."

"You must have had a wretched time all evening."

"No, I really had a very good time. I think Jeanne's perfectly swell, and I liked Dave Fulton, though I didn't think I was going to. And I simply loved the music. But I'm afraid I must have seemed pretty subdued. It wasn't a very brilliant first appearance for your young fiancée."

"You were splendid," he said. "I was just as proud as I could be." And now, indeed, as he looked back on the party and remembered Daphne among all those people, the whole evening took on a brighter, warmer tone.

He recalled how charming she had looked when he first came in, standing beside Edwin at the far end of the room, so brown and slim in her white dress, her lovely long neck bent forward, her thick brown hair sweeping back from her temples to her shoulders. The lamp on the piano beside her had emphasized the modeling of her rather high cheekbones but left her eyes in shadow—long eyes which, from where he stood, he might have thought were brown if he had not known and loved their clear slate color. She had been smiling, faintly amused at Edwin, but no one but himself, he thought, would have noticed the suggestion of an upper curl at each end of her mouth.

He tightened his arm about her waist.

"You know, Daphne," he said, "I don't think that even yet you have an idea of what you mean to me. You're so awfully modest. You've had so little experience. It seems almost unfair that I should take advantage of your youth and marry you when you're hardly out of college."

"And yet you keep urging me to marry you and get it over with," she said. "How do you account for that?"

"It's easily accounted for," he said, "but I don't approve of it. I think you're quite right to put me through my paces first."

She laughed. "Not at all!" she exclaimed. "It's more like waiting until my eyes are no longer dazzled so that I can actually see what I'm getting. And it's not because of my youth, you decrepit old man! How old are you, anyway? Thirty-four?"

"But seriously," he went on, "you've no idea how attractive you are. All kinds of men would fall in love with you sooner or later, if you'd only give them the chance."

"Is this just a very polite way," she asked, "of calling the whole thing off?"

"Don't you dare try it," he said; and for an instant, at the mere thought of losing her, of the emptiness, the awful restlessness, he felt a stab of anguish. "But do you know— and this is the actual truth—until I ran across you last winter I'd firmly made up my mind that I'd never marry? That shows what you did to me, and when you think of all the good-looking coeds that have consulted me about their psyches for the last few years, you ought to feel pretty damn flattered."

"Flattered! I should say I do. But why were you so down on marriage?"

"I wasn't down on marriage. Only marriage for me. I've always been a bit suspicious of women. I just thought I'd never fall in love. I didn't think I had it in me. When I was young I used to be rather a strange kind of cuss—sort of morbid and lonely. I used to read a lot, but I didn't think people used to like me. I didn't think I could get on with them."

"I've never known anyone that more people like," she said, "or anyone that gets on better with people—that is when you're with them."

He smiled. "Just what do you mean by that?" he asked. "Of course it sounds like nonsense, but as a matter of fact I think it's rather penetrating."

"What I mean is . . ." She hesitated. "It's rather hard to put into words. I mean that when you're with people anyone might think that you were a born mixer; but when you're alone, I mean alone with me, I could easily think sometimes that you wouldn't get on at all, that you didn't like them so terribly, that you almost resented them or at least that you were sort of shy. I don't mean shy with *me*, you understand. . . ."

"I understand perfectly," he said, "and it only means that I show you my real self. I can use that nice old-fashioned expression since none of my colleagues are around.

32

But I'm glad if you do see me as I really am, Daphne, because no one can see himself, not even a psychologist, and
if you're not too far wrong and can still put up with me,
I must be worth salvaging. I will say, though, that I'd have
plenty of excuse for being queer."

"You're not queer," she exclaimed. "You're not nearly so
queer as I am, Harold."

"We'll let that pass," he said. "Did I ever tell you about
my grandparents? I lived with them after my father and
mother died. They were both very religious. They had a
firm belief in eternal damnation, and they loved to take it
out on me. I had a little room alone in the attic, and there
were two prints that used to hang on the stairs, so that I'd
have to pass them every time I went up or down. If I close
my eyes I can see them now, just as plainly as ever. The
first one represented two figures playing cards; one was
dressed in white and the other in black, and you couldn't
see either of their faces. The other print showed the same
two figures, only the one in white had its head flung down
on the table, among the scattered cards, and the one in
black was standing up, with arms raised as if it was about
to spring. Its hood was flung back, and you could see a great
face, blood-red, and with the most diabolical expression,
you can take my word for it, absolutely gloating over the
other one. They were supposed to represent the struggle for
the soul of man, and I used to feel my way up and down
stairs with my eyes closed, so that I wouldn't have to look
at them."

"You poor boy!" Daphne exclaimed. "I can just imagine
them. But why didn't you ask your grandparents to take
them down?"

"Ask them!" he said. "I used to plead with them, but
they wouldn't do it. They thought those prints were good
medicine. Certainly the flavor lasted. *Ma jeunesse ne fut
qu'un ténébreux orage.*"

"What's that?" she asked curiously. *"Ma jeunesse . . .
my youth . . ."*

"It's a line from Baudelaire. 'My youth was nothing but
a murky storm,' or something like that. I was quite proud
when I came across it in sophomore French, because I

thought it applied especially to me—me and Baudelaire."

He felt her hand pressed suddenly to his where it clasped her waist; and as he thought of the difference between then and now, between now and even a year ago, when he had been rejected by the Army and did not yet know Daphne, such a surge of thankfulness swept over him, of comfort, of faith in the future, that he could hardly trust himself to speak. It seemed to him that Daphne was all the health, the naturalness, the loving-kindness in the world.

The moonlight through the trees had grown clearer. It had lost its rusty tint and now suggested motionless gray water shot through with a vague phosphorescence. He stopped and pulled her close against him; then pushed her softly away and put his hands on her shoulders.

"Let me look at you," he said. "Let me see if I can really make out your face."

He could see her eyes staring into his, her full firm lips smiling and yet serious. In a moment he would feel the warmth of those lips.

That at least is what he could have sworn the instant before. But now, more abruptly than the cry of the whippoorwill, stabbing the silence of the moonlight, there came a scream that rose quavering and awful, higher, higher, unbearable, and then stopped short before it reached its climax.

Daphne pressed close against him. Rigid himself, he could feel her body trembling all through.

"What was it?" she exclaimed half sobbing. "Oh what was it?"

"Something not very nice, I guess," he muttered. "Wait a second!" Then as loud as he could, he shouted: "We're coming! We'll be right there!"

He stroked her shoulders gently. "Do you think you can follow me?" he asked. "It's off there to the right. It can't be far. We must get there at once. You stay a little behind me, but don't get too far away . . . not under any circumstances."

CHAPTER V

*D*APHNE was glad she had to run so fast, pushing
branches out of the way, trying not to trip over
fallen trees, because it prevented her from thinking, almost
from feeling. Twigs snapped, boughs swished as Harold
pounded on ahead, making as much noise as he could.
Dusty leaves brushed her face, like the powdery wings of
moths; briars caught at her ankles, and for an instant, in-
congruously, she found herself thinking that her nylon
stockings must be ruined.

Then, with a flash of terror like the sudden twinge of a
tooth, she thought that she had lost Harold. The crashing
noises had stopped. She could see nothing ahead but the
tangle of shadows, the cobwebby pools of light, and between
two branches the gnawed disc of the moon.

"Harold," she called breathlessly. "Harold, where are
you?"

"It's all right." His voice came from close at hand. "I've
found her. I think we scared him off in time. She's not
dead."

Then she saw him stooping, on his knees, not thirty feet
away. As she hurried toward him she could hear a faint
whimpering such as a sick child might make in its sleep, and
could see that he was bending over the body of a girl or
woman who lay on her face at the edge of a road which
divided this part of the wood from what looked like a patch
of victory gardens. Beyond this open space she could see
lights in windows, and a street lamp shining through trees.
From the direction of the houses there came the yelping of
a dog.

"There, there," Harold murmured. "He's gone. You're
among friends now. You're quite safe."

He looked over his shoulder at Daphne. "She doesn't
hear me," he said. "As far as I can make out she was
stabbed in her left arm; I think that's all. I suppose he was
trying for her heart. It doesn't seem bad, though of course

35

you can't tell. But the poor girl is literally half crazy with fright."

"I should think she would be," Daphne said. "Do you think it was . . . he?"

"I guess he's the one, all right. Apparently we weren't talking such nonsense as I thought at dinner."

Daphne stooped down beside him and tried to see just how badly the arm had been slashed. Now that she could help this poor whimpering girl whose terror she could so well imagine, her own fear had left her.

"Have you got a match, Harold?" she asked—"and a knife? I think we'd better cut away the sleeve."

Harold gave her his pocketknife and struck a match which he cupped in his hands while Daphne ripped open the blood-soaked cotton. She had a glimpse of a long dark gash from which blood was welling, like water from a spring, before the match went out, and for an instant she could distinguish nothing. Then as her eyes grew adjusted once more to the moonlight she could see clearly enough to work.

"We must stop the blood," she said. "I think the brachial artery must be cut. Will you hold her arm for a minute? Here, let me show you where to put your fingers. But you probably know much more about it than I do."

"Indeed I don't," Harold said. "I'm at your orders."

She guided his hand as accurately as she could to "the point of digital pressure" she had learned in her first-aid course, and to her relief the flow of blood dwindled to a trickle. Then, with Harold's knife, she cut a long piece from the bottom of her slip.

"Have you got a pencil?" she asked. "A fairly long one?"

"A pencil?"

"Yes, to make a tourniquet," she explained; and after a minute's work, she felt that at least the girl would not bleed to death.

"You're wonderful," Harold said. "The sight of blood is apt to flurry me a bit—or perhaps it's the smell. That's a fine thing for a scientist to admit, isn't it? But now we ought to have a doctor, and of course the police, though I doubt if they can do much good. Damn it, I wish I knew what to do! I hardly like to pick her up and carry her be-

36

cause there may be something else wrong with her. I certainly don't want to leave you here with her alone, and I hate to send you across those gardens."

"Of course I can go," Daphne said. "I won't be nervous —really. It's only a few hundred yards."

"No, wait a moment," he said. "I don't think it will be necessary. Here comes someone from that nearest house." And Daphne could see a flashlight moving toward them.

"The thing is," Harold went on, in a tense hurried voice, "I'm afraid this may not count."

"May not count?" she repeated. "What do you mean?"

"I'm afraid he may have been interrupted too soon."

"How could it be too soon?"

"I mean too soon from his point of view. To embark on an attack like this must require an enormous urge, an enormous excitement. The emotional relief must be correspondingly great. But I don't believe he got it this time. It was like snatching food from the mouth of a starving man."

"Do you mean," she asked, and she felt faintly sick, "that he may be trying it again? You mean quite soon?"

"I have no idea. We may have given him such a shock that he'll never try again. This may not even be the same man, for all we know. But just for my own peace of mind I didn't like the idea of your walking alone through those cabbages. In this moonlight you can see why they call them 'heads,' can't you?"

He rose to his feet as the man with the flashlight crossed the road. He was an elderly man with a beard; a stout woman hurried close behind him.

"What was that screeching?" she asked. "You be careful now. My man's got a gun."

"A girl has been attacked," Harold said, and his voice was all at once so natural that it made Daphne realize how strained it had been. "She's bleeding, but I don't think it's serious. Your husband can stay here with me, if I seem like a suspicious character, but please hurry back and call the Woodside General Hospital. And then call the police. Tell them it's urgent. And wait a moment. I wish you'd also call Dr. Terrence Macfarlane. The number is Woodland 124."

It seemed to Daphne that the police would never arrive, though Harold told her later that actually the car had driven up just eleven minutes after the woman left them. Daphne had sat down among the dry grass and weeds and gently lifted the girl's head on to her lap. The girl herself was quiet now, and Daphne was sure that she was only half conscious. The moon, well above the trees, glared down from the empty sky; the dog was still barking beyond the gardens, and the bearded man stood suspiciously a few yards away, as if afraid to let them out of his sight or to come too near them.

It was only when the police car stopped beside them, and the ambulance drove up a moment later, that she realized how nervously exhausted she was. She was thankful that the officer let Harold do most of the explaining because if she had had to talk much herself she would have burst into tears. The man was very polite, she had to admit, but in her present mood she could imagine that the smoothness of his manner covered the darkest suspicion and was merely a device to entrap them. It was a relief when Terry arrived in his car perhaps ten minutes later and hailed the officer in charge by his first name.

When at last, at about midnight, Harold saw her up-stairs to her apartment (thank heaven Terry had been there to drive them in!), she was too tired to dread being left alone, and wanted nothing in the world but the chance to sleep.

She was wakened by the telephone jangling in her ears, and knew it had been ringing and ringing. She jumped up and hurried to answer it but by the time she took off the receiver there was no one on the line.

The room was speckled with sunlight, and glancing at her watch she saw to her amazement that it was twenty-five minutes past ten. It must have been Harold calling her. He had classes from ten-thirty until one-thirty in the naval training program; she had to be at the hospital at one, but she would see him as usual at dinner. It was probably too late for her to go down to the Red Cross workroom this morning to fold bandages, and she still felt tired.

She walked on to the little iron balcony outside her bedroom window ,and looked down over the lake through the thin boughs of the hickory that half shaded the room. Not a leaf stirred; the end of a small branch was muffled by a caterpillar nest, as if the sweepings of a broom had been tangled among the twigs. There was a haze over the pale water and the hills beyond. The sky seemed charged with an infinite reserve of heat which little by little through the day would seep down to bake the earth even harder, to shrivel the grass, to wilt the leaves, to numb the energy and exasperate the nerves of animals and people.

Daphne ran the bathtub half full and lay in it for at least ten minutes. Then she made herself a cup of coffee and wrote a long letter to Barbara. "At least," she thought, "I should be thankful that I don't have to drill all day in the sun, or crawl through swamps the way poor Jimmy may be doing."

She described her last night's adventure in detail. It was a relief to write about it, to make it sound scary and yet somewhat amusing, like a good horror film: it made it seem further away, a thing complete in itself which she should not have to think of again.

When she reached the hospital she was assigned to the women's surgical ward, and she was finishing her first alcohol rub when Terry Macfarlane came quietly up beside her.

"Well," he asked, "how did you survive last evening? That final act wasn't meant to be on the program. Too sensational."

She looked over her shoulder and smiled, delighted to see him, even a little proud that he should find her prosaically at work. "I survived beautifully," she said. "The first part was such fun it made me forget the last."

"You must have a poor memory," he exclaimed. "The girl is here in this ward, you know—the last bed down there on the left. Her upper arm was pretty badly slashed, and I had to mess around with her for awhile. We're keeping her a few days for observation. Wouldn't you like to go see her?"

"I would very much," Daphne said, and wondered why she felt so excited.

39

She followed him to the end of the ward where they stopped before the girl's bed. "Hullo, Margaret," he said, "this is Daphne Gray. She was with the fellow that saved you from the Big Bad Wolf. Daphne, this is Margaret Peterson."

The girl was dark-haired, rather heavy, with a round sensible face. She smiled cordially at Daphne. "Tell your boy friend I'm sure glad he was around," she exclaimed. "I guess I must be pretty lucky."

"How do you feel now?" Daphne asked.

"Oh my arm doesn't bother me so much," she said, "but it's not what you'd call a pleasant memory."

"Well, you girls have a good time," Terry said. "I thought you ought to have something in common."

"I must get on too," Daphne said. "There's lots to be done." But she found herself lingering.

She was surprised that she did feel she had so much in common with this girl: it was as if they had mysteriously been placed in the same category, as if they were two sisters branded and set apart. Then it occurred to her that there was a third sister who was no longer here.

"It must have been horrible," she said. "I'm surprised you can be so calm this afternoon."

"Well, it's over now," Margaret said, "but it just about scared me out of ten years' growth. I'd been out to mail a letter, and then it was so hot I thought I'd take a stroll around the garden field to get a look at the moon. I thought I heard the leaves rustling a bit but I didn't pay much attention, and then something sprang out on me like a great big monkey, but of course I knew it was a man. Lucky for me I'm fairly husky, because I shook him off, and boy did I run! I could hear his breathing when he came after me, like a great suction pump, and then I must have let out that yell. I don't remember the rest. It's funny, I don't recollect being stabbed at all."

At five o'clock that afternoon, when Daphne went off duty, Dave Fulton walked up to her in the dark hospital lobby. "Hullo!" he said. "This *is* a surprise!"

She looked at him suspiciously. "For me, at any rate."

"Well, I thought I'd sort of drop around and see how you were. How about going somewhere for a cocktail?"

"No thanks," she said. "I had enough last night."

"Well then a malted milk or some ice cream. We can go to that drugstore across the street on the corner."

He looked rather different from last evening: no longer so conventionally handsome. It must have been the brilliance of his eyes and teeth, his general air of darkness, alertness, and neatness, that had given her her first impression. She saw now that his nose was too large, that his smile was a little crooked: it made him look nicer, and certainly far more reliable. "I think a malted milk would be very good," she said. "I didn't eat much lunch."

The air-conditioned drugstore felt like a cave underground. He led her to a booth in one of the back corners and gave their orders to the girl.

"That was a mean business last night," he said. "They had an account in this afternoon's paper. It's a damn shame you had to be mixed up in it. It must have given you a terrific wallop."

"Well, after all," she said not quite sincerely, "I see things every day here in the hospital . . ."

"Of course you do, but you don't have maniacs running around loose in the corridors. Damn it, if I'd come along a bit sooner I might have had a chance of nabbing that bird. That's what comes of being a perfect gentleman. I gave you and Harold too much of a start."

"Did you walk home?" she asked. "Couldn't you get a ride with the Hatfields?"

"I've no doubt I could," he said, "but I felt like walking."

"On so hot a night?"

"What about you?" he asked. "You walked yourself."

"I had company."

"Don't rub it in!" he exclaimed. "Do you remember when I barged into you on the porch with that highball, and you told me you wanted to be alone and quiet for a bit so that you could remember how beautiful the music was? Well, that's something the way I felt after you had gone."

She was glad that the girl came up just then with their
41

malted milks. She could not help feeling pleased at such a charming compliment, but it embarrassed her a little. Perhaps her own manner had been too forward; perhaps without meaning to she had been leading him on.

"I hope the police didn't rout out Harold this morning!" she said. "They said they might keep in touch with him." She shuddered. "I hate being mixed up with the police!"

"You haven't seen Harold today?"

"No. I slept till half-past ten. Wasn't that awful? Then he had a whole string of classes. But he's coming to dinner with me tonight."

"As I think I remarked before," he said, with one of his sudden smiles, "lucky Harold!"

When they walked out of the door, the heat fell fiercely upon them, and Daphne had to squint in the glare.

"Good-by," she said. "Thanks a lot. I've got some shopping I must do."

She was grateful to him for not offering to go with her.

It was nearly six o'clock when Harold appeared at her apartment. His blond hair was tousled as usual; he looked very hot; but his eyes were glowing and alert. His face was transfigured by the restless energy which, when it seized him, made him seem to her so much more alive than anyone else she knew. She flung her arms around him, for she had rarely been more delighted to see him.

"I hardly dared show my face in here," he said, "after that darn fool telephone call this morning. When it kept ringing I knew you must be asleep, but I just wanted to say hullo before my classes. I woke you up of course?"

"It was about time," she said. "I didn't fold my bandages, as it was. They didn't come to see you again, did they?"

"Who's 'they'?"

"The police."

He laughed. "Good Lord no! We're not under suspicion, dearest. It would be much better if we were. Did you notice how that fellow lost interest in us the moment I established my identity as a respectable citizen? They ought to realize that in a crime like this, respectability, position, etc., are completely irrelevant."

42

"I saw the girl today in the hospital," Daphne told him. "She seems very nice and very sensible."

"Good for her!" Harold exclaimed. "Lots of girls would be jittery for months after such an experience."

"And now," Daphne suggested, "you might make a cocktail, that is if you'd like one."

"I would very much, if you'll have one too."

"I'd love one," she said. "I declined one this afternoon, so I'd be ready to have one with you."

"Is Terry trying to make an alcoholic out of you?" he asked as she followed him into the small kitchen. "I'll have to speak to him."

'It wasn't Terry. It was Dave Fulton. You know, Harold, he told me that last night he was walking not so very far behind us."

"Humph!" Harold exclaimed. "That's interesting."

"If he'd only been there ten minutes sooner, he thought there might have been a chance of his getting the man. I certainly wish he had."

"Yes," Harold said grimly. "So do I."

As he mixed the cocktails, Daphne was taking things from the icebox.

"There's nothing hot tonight," she said. "I hope you don't mind. I've got salmon, mayonnaise, and deviled eggs, and potato chips, and there's peach shortcake for dessert."

He whistled. "I'm glad I didn't eat any lunch."

They ate their dinner in the kitchen, and afterwards sat together in the living room, for Daphne felt too tired and hot to go dancing or even to a movie. From the lake there floated up clearly the voices of people canoeing; and the hooting of a little owl was repeated from the trees in the gardens along the shore.

"You know, Daphne," Harold said abruptly, "I don't want to be always harping on this unknown murderer, but if they ever want to run him down, I think they should have the help of a psychologist. It was obvious last night that they took it for granted he must be some kind of roughneck, whether he was mad or sane. They'll be hauling in poor innocent transients, or soldiers A.W.O.L. They'll be working, in so far as they do anything, from the crime back

43

to the criminal; and unless I'm very much mistaken, they won't find anything to go on. That won't get them anywhere. I'm going to offer my services. I think if I go about it in the right way, they will be grateful for help."

"Oh no," Daphne exclaimed, "you mustn't do that, Harold! Please don't! For my sake." She was surprised herself that she shrank so violently from the idea.

He smiled. "Why not? There couldn't be the slightest danger."

"But it's not that. It's just the thought of your being connected with such a horrible thing. I want to forget it. I'd hate to have to think that every time I saw you you'd been talking it all over, and snooping around with police detectives, perhaps. I want to get as far away from it as I possibly can."

"But Daphne darling," he said, "I wouldn't mention it to you, if you'd rather I didn't. You certainly agree it's important that he should be caught, if only for the sake of possible future victims. And I honestly think I could be of help. I've been brooding over it all day, considering possibilities. I dreamed of it most of last night. I can't get it out of my mind."

"I don't care," she exclaimed, and now there were tears in her voice. "I know it's unreasonable, but I can't help feeling that way. I feel it very strongly, and I don't see how you could really help them. It's just because you like to be mixed up in it, from a psychological point of view. It's just your morbid curiosity. But Harold, promise me you won't. Promise me you'll just let it alone. Will you promise?"

"But darling, if I felt it was my duty . . . as a citizen . . ."

To her shame, she burst into tears. "I think you're mean," she sobbed. "This is the first thing I've ever asked you to do, and you won't do it. I should think you might see how I feel. I'm so upset. I'm on edge. I hate the whole business so. I just hate it, and I hate breaking down like this!"

"Dearest, you mustn't . . . Daphne, you make me feel so cruel . . ."

He took her in his arms, and she could feel his strong

hands gently, coaxingly, trying to soothe her tense and shaken body. "Of course we won't speak of it again, if that's the way you feel. But you seemed so calm and cheerful."

"Yes, I was," she said through her tears. "I thought I was . . . until all of a sudden . . ."

She was calm again when she kissed him good-by and listened to him walking down the stairs, but her nose was stopped up from crying; and she felt resentful both of herself and of Harold.

When she returned from the tiny hall into the living room, it seemed breathlessly quiet. There were no longer voices on the lake. The white walls, the cretonne-covered furniture, the water color of tulips above the mantel, all these things that she knew so well might have been changed by the heat and the silence into something not themselves.

Then faintly she heard footsteps coming up the stairs. She wondered, if they stopped before her door, if there should be a knock, whether she would dare open it; but they passed by on their way to the third floor and again there was perfect stillness. It seemed as if she could actually feel it vibrating, or was it the heat? Then she realized that it was the perpetual faint sound of the crickets, that had followed her here, that had been with her all day; and suddenly she began to tremble. It was absurd, a purely physical reaction, like the twitching of an eyelid, but for several minutes she could not make herself stop.

She undressed at once and lay down on her bed, but for a long time she could not go to sleep; and when she did she kept dreaming that she was wandering through an endless gray wood. There were cobwebs between the trees that it took all her strength to push through . . . and yet she had to break through them to escape what was stalking her . . . far away as yet, but that did not deceive her. Because she had been here before, and this time it was a little nearer . . . because she knew that she would be here again; that it would be waiting for her, next time a little nearer still . . . a little nearer . . . and always a little nearer . . .

CHAPTER VI .

*D*URING the next week Daphne resumed her usual way of life: folding bandages in the mornings, going to the hospital in the afternoons. Three times Dave was waiting for her in the lobby, and she felt it had become almost an accepted thing that she should go with him to the drugstore for a cold drink. One night there had been a violent thundershower, but the water had rolled off the hard ground, and the next morning the heat was as oppressive as ever. Each evening Harold and she had dinner together. Sometimes she would cook it at home, but more often he would take her to a restaurant; and twice they had gone dancing, though she could not really enjoy it.

In spite of herself she was jumpy and depressed. She felt that perhaps she was working too hard at the hospital, that it might be wiser to go there only three afternoons a week, at least until cooler weather set in, but she could not bear to think of the empty hours. It was partly, she knew, because she could not sleep satisfactorily. When she went to bed she would try to read, and then the book would slip from her hands in a few minutes and her eyes would close sometimes before she even put out the light; but before very long she would wake up after confused and tiring dreams that she could not exactly remember, and then it would be several hours before she could fall asleep again.

Harold had been very good about the whole thing. Although his manner, at once intense and abstracted, made her suspect that the attack was still on his mind, he did not refer to it, and she felt almost guilty that she had exacted his promise. She thought it probable that he also was working too hard. His teaching schedule with the Naval Reserve was very heavy, and she knew he was putting in several hours a day in his laboratory. It seemed to her that he was living on his nerves: he would arrive at her apartment restless and fidgeting, and only settle down after he had drunk a couple of cocktails.

A strange idea kept haunting her mind at all hours of the day and night. It was not Margaret but herself that the murderer had first pursued; she had upset his plans by suspecting his presence and walking so very fast, or perhaps in the daylight he had not quite dared attack her. Margaret had been merely a substitute; but this had not succeeded either, and now he would return to the victim of his first choice. In daylight, in the presence of people, the whole thing often seemed fantastic, and if it alarmed her it was merely as a symptom of her nervous condition; but more and more, especially at night, it would come over her with the logic of a mathematical proof. She would lie open-eyed in the airless darkness of her bedroom, and feel that she was doomed, with the same incredulous and hopeless certainty that had seized her one summer as a little girl when for some forgotten reason she was convinced that she had contracted leprosy.

On Friday afternoon, just a week after the dinner party, she was sitting down to lunch at a small restaurant on the square when Professor Hatfield came up to her table.

"How do you do?" he said. "May I join you?"

"Of course," she answered. "That would be very nice," and she was really glad of his company, for she had come to dread being alone.

"If I may offer a suggestion," he said, "I should advise your ordering the fresh shrimps with cheese. It's about the best thing they have. Of course we have no really choice restaurants in town, but I've tried little by little to discover the best things they serve at each one, and also the special things to avoid. I must admit the second list is far longer than the first."

"I should love some shrimps," she said, and he gave the order.

As they ate, she brought up the subject of birds, and for a time he told her in his quiet, overprecise manner about the various warblers that came through in the spring.

"There's a small owl that I can hear from my room," she said presently. "I don't know why they are associated with witches and ghosts. I always love to hear him. He seems like company when I lie awake."

47

"I'm devoted to owls," he said. "I used to keep them until my wife objected. I argued for a time and then decided it just wasn't worth the trouble. By the way, the night of our dinner party last week, when you had that really unfortunate experience, I tracked down the most charming little screech owl. I heard him just after we left Terry's, only a few hundred yards from the gate, in fact. I made Wanda let me out, much to her disgust, while I trailed him. I finally found the little fellow on a branch no higher than my head. He let me come within a yard of him, and then for at least a minute we just stared at each other. It was light enough by that time for me to see him quite well. He was in the brown phase not the gray. The only trouble was that I had to walk home, and you remember how warm it was that evening—not that it's grown much cooler since. After our talk at dinner Wanda refused to wait alone in the parked car. I'm afraid she may have counted on Dave Fulton's company. Of course the event proved that her nervousness was not entirely unfounded."

"But wasn't Edwin with you?" Daphne asked.

"No. He said he was restless after playing. He wanted to walk, to look at the moon. But you know, he's rather a queer duck. Temperamental. My own private opinion is that, knowing my habits, he suspected he might be left alone with Wanda, and I think he's just a little afraid of her." He chuckled confidentially. "In fact, I think he's a wee bit shy of women generally. Young men, I'm afraid, sometimes find Wanda's manner a trifle . . . shall I say predatory? That is, if they don't know her well, of course."

He chuckled again, with the odd impersonality of a demure yet possibly ribald old parrot, and Daphne could not decide whether his final phrase was ironic.

That evening she would have told Harold of her special obsession, if she had not felt it would be silly to bring up the subject herself when she had made him promise not to have anything to do with it. The moment he had said good night, however, she felt that the really silly thing was to let such a scruple hold her back. She remembered her childhood fear of leprosy and how it was put to flight in a few minutes

48

when she had at last, through sheer misery, dared to mention it to her father. The next morning, as she had breakfast with Harold on the Union Terrace, with the cheerful lake in front of her and students at the tables near by, she rather shamefacedly confessed her special worry. "Now go ahead and laugh at me," she said. "I know I deserve it."

"I certainly won't laugh at you," he said. "I can understand only too well how such a thing might get into your head, and you simply wouldn't be able to get it out. Has it occurred to you that in this heat there seems to be no air, no breathing space, you might say, for ideas to escape into, and so they just keep grinding around inside your brain? But you must believe me when I say there is absolutely nothing to this substitute idea. There really isn't. You're not a marked woman, my dear. I'd have put you on your guard if I thought you were. As a matter of fact, the police are keeping a pretty sharp lookout. Why only yesterday Inspector Waters was saying . . ."

Daphne put down her coffee cup.

"The police!" she exclaimed. "Have you been going to the police? Have you been working with them, Harold?"

He flushed, his eyes slid sidewise to avoid hers, and she could see that he had been taken unawares.

"Well, not really working *with* them," he said after an uneasy moment.

"But Harold, you promised me you'd have absolutely nothing to do with it. I believed you. I even felt rather guilty. I never dreamed that you were up to your ears in it all along. If you lied to me, how can I ever believe what you say?"

"My dear Daphne," he said, "to be exact, I didn't promise I wouldn't help, if I could. I only promised you we'd not talk about it, you and I. I chose my words at the time very carefully so I wouldn't have to lie to you. And it was you that brought it up just now, remember."

"You chose your words carefully!" she exclaimed, so fiercely that two boys at the next table looked around and she knew that she must lower her voice. "Yes, you chose your words carefully to keep within the literal truth, perhaps, and all the time you were deceiving me. You knew

49

how I felt! You knew I trusted you completely. Well, I've learned my lesson!"

She felt furiously angry and hurt; there were tears in her eyes; and the suspicion that she might be unfair only added to her anger. It almost seemed to her, fantastically, that it was Harold's connection with the case that had infected her with its deadly atmosphere: he had brought it into her rooms each time he entered them; its miasma had spread from him, from his mind, his clothes, his hands, to saturate her own thoughts and her dreams.

He rose now, suddenly very pale, from the table.

"Daphne," he said, "you must let me explain. I said I wasn't really working *with* them. . . ."

"It makes no difference," she said hotly, feeling it was somehow cowardly on his part that there should be other people around to prevent the full release of her anger. "It's just quibbling. Well, it simply means that there's no one at all I can count on."

"Daphne, you can always count on me . . . Daphne, darling . . ."

"I'm not your darling," she exclaimed. "And don't dare to follow me. I feel as if I'd never like to see you again. It may be different tomorrow. I don't know."

And she almost ran off the terrace, feeling that everyone was staring at her, that her face was red and swollen, that she must not burst into tears—not until she was alone.

She was walking along the Lake Drive half an hour later, wretched and still angry, when a man on a bay horse cantered past her, pulled up a few yards ahead, and turned back. Then she recognized Dave, and though she hated to see anyone at this moment she forced herself to smile.

"This is wonderful," he exclaimed. "It's the first time this week I've even had a glimpse of you that wasn't premeditated. How's everything?"

"Not so good," she said, "if you really want to know."

"I'm sorry," he said with sudden earnestness, and dismounted beside her. "What's the matter? Could I help in any way?"

"No one can help," she told him. "And it's not important. I'm just in a bad mood, that's all. I often am."

She turned her head away from him so that he would not see that she had been crying, and stared over the fringe of reeds with dried foam caught among their stems, like flakes of dirty soapsuds. Beyond them, a hundred feet out on the muddy greenish water, a young man was paddling a red canoe, with a girl resting on pillows in the bow.

"An idea occurs to me," Dave said. "I think it's swell, and I hope you will. Tomorrow's Sunday. I have all day off and so do you. What do you say we get us a canoe and paddle across the lake with our lunch? I know a place you'll love. It's an absolute money-back guarantee."

Daphne wondered whether he guessed she had had a quarrel with Harold. Perhaps he had, but it made no difference. If Harold should object, it served him right.

"I'd love to go," she said. "Do you want me to bring anything?"

"Now come!" he exclaimed. "Don't be insulting. I have my pride, though you might not suspect it."

She felt that her eyes were again filling with tears.

"And now you must go," she said, "or next thing I'll be cross with *you*, and there won't be any picnic."

"You certainly have the knack of getting rid of a guy," he said. "Watch me!" He mounted, touched his horse's flanks, and bounded away from her like the hero of a Western thriller.

She ate no lunch that day, and had to keep scolding herself at the hospital for being so cross with the patients. Ten minutes after she reached home Harold telephoned her.

"Daphne," he begged, "won't you let me come around now? I thought we might go out to the Shack for some fried chicken."

"No thanks," she answered coldly, "I'm not hungry."

"Well at least won't you let me see you? Won't you let me explain?"

"No," she repeated. "When I want to see you I'll let you know."

"Tomorrow morning?"

"I'll be busy tomorrow. Good-by."

She hung up sharply, because she felt that if she kept him on the line any longer she might relent; but her eyes blurred again, as they had done several times during the day. She did not bother to cook any supper, but took merely some bread and butter, a peach, and a glass of milk.

She turned out her light at nine o'clock, and perhaps because her temper had exhausted her she went to sleep almost at once. She had no idea how late it was when she woke, but there was no sound of voices from the lake, and no sign of dawn in the sky that she could see through the branches outside her window. She had a strange feeling that she should not have awakened: this was not like her usual wakings in the night, when she emerged slowly through a sticky hot surface of dreams which did not entirely dissolve until she opened her eyes. Tonight she had been aroused from a deep sleep; there had been something. . . . Could the telephone have rung? But no, she would have recognized that even through sleep. Could anyone have knocked at the door?

And then it came again: a strange scratching or scuffling, a dry spasmodic rustle. It was outside her window. It was in the hickory tree. Some animal? But she knew, as if a cold hand had suddenly squeezed her heart, that it was not an animal.

She felt that if she ever were going to move from her bed she must do so at once, before all her strength oozed from her. She sat up, put her feet to the floor. For an instant it seemed to be rocking beneath her. She must overcome that feeling or she would never reach the window.

Thank heaven there were shutters! The noise outside continued, with brief pauses. It grew slightly louder. Someone was climbing the tree.

She walked across the room, and stood for a moment just inside the window, at the edge of the white curtain. She would have to open the screen door and step out on the balcony to reach the blinds. Then she would have to stoop to release the metal clamps that held them firm against the outside wall of the building. Would it be better to turn on the light, to let it be known that she was awake? She stared out through a chink between the window frame and the curtain, and yes, surely, there close to the trunk, on a branch hardly below the level of the balcony, she could see a huddled mass; she could see quite distinctly an arm groping upwards.

As if compelled by something outside herself, she stepped on to the balcony, bent down, released the fastenings and pulled the blinds together. Then she stepped back, drew the bolt in the middle, reached for the top one, and bent a second time to push the bottom one into its hole. In the blacked-out room, she felt her way to the light switch beside her dressing table and turned on the light.

The noise had stopped for a moment; but she heard it again: a rustling, a sudden slithering, and then a thud as something hit the ground.

She drew her breath, swayed, caught herself, ran to her bed, knocking against a chair on the way, and pulled the sheet over her head as she used to do when she was a little girl.

CHAPTER VII

*W*HEN Daphne woke up, she thought for a moment that it was still night, and that she had been dreaming, but then she realized that the room was dark because the blinds were closed, and that her experience was real. Turning on the light by her bed, she saw that it was nearly nine o'clock. Splinters of sun pierced the chinks in the shutters. "Did it really happen the way I remember it?" she wondered.

She crossed the room, unfastened the blinds, and stepped on to the balcony. A number of hickory twigs were broken and dangling, and by peering over the railing she could see that near the ground a strip of the loose shaggy bark had been torn off.

The air was bright and dry, and for the first time in days there was a faint breeze; a spark would flash here and there across the surface of the lake as if a leaping fish had caught the sunlight. She remembered thankfully her picnic with Dave. If he had not been coming she would have had to telephone Harold, because she could not bear to be alone today. She was no longer angry; she felt that she had acted like a child; but she still did not want to give in too soon.

One thing was certain, however: she would not sleep another night in this room until the murderer was caught. In her dressing gown she walked across the hall and tapped on the door of the apartment opposite, where Mary Sharpe and Gertrude McNeill lived. They were assistants in English, and although she felt they were overserious, with the peculiar glazed nearsighted eyes that she associated with women Ph.D's, she liked them both and saw them fairly often. When Mary came to the door, Daphne told her of her last night's experience, and asked if she could sleep on their sitting room divan for a few nights.

Mary was thrilled, and insisted on dragging Gertrude out of bed to hear the adventure. "Of course you can sleep in the living room as long as you like," she exclaimed. "It won't have to be on the divan either, because we've got an army cot where Gerty's sister sleeps when she stays with us."

Daphne agreed to this, if they would let her fold up the cot every morning and put it away.

"It's awfully narrow," Gertrude warned her, "and I'm sure it's not nearly so comfortable as your own bed."

"At least there are no trees outside your windows," Daphne said, "and just now that's the most important thing for me, as far as sleeping comfort is concerned."

Dave called for her at half-past eleven, with a knapsack slung over his shoulders. It was a shabby old knapsack, bulging with supplies; she could see the handle of a skillet and the tops of two thermos bottles protruding; and yet, the way he wore it, it had an air of extraordinary jauntiness. As she shook his hand she wondered whether she should tell him about last night, but decided she would not: if she did, it would only mean talking about it, and it was the last thing she wanted to have recalled.

As they glided away from the university pier, Daphne, in spite of last night's experience, was more cheerful than she had been in several days. Perhaps it was the new tremor of life in the air, the little gusts of freshness that she could see approaching in dark arrowy sweeps across the water before she felt them on her face and arms; or it may have been because now, as she looked lazily backwards from her

54

comfortable pillow, the whole town dropped away from her, grew small and neat and innocent—the houses among their trees, the church spires, and even the red-brick high-shouldered mass of Science Hall that dominated the campus, and that always had seemed to her rather sinister in its towering ugliness.

When she mentioned this to Dave, he laughed.

"I'd hate to have you think that," he said. "My office is way up at the very top, in one of those queer little gables. And of course Harold's is on the second floor, but that's not nearly so nice. I wouldn't change mine for any other place on the whole campus."

"But isn't that where they keep the cadavers?" she asked. "I thought that was where the med students did their dissecting."

"You're right," he said. "But it's all very cozy and sort of old-fashioned. The whole top of the building is a regular labyrinth, with passages you almost have to stoop to get through, and little private dissecting rooms with no windows, nothing but skylights; and there's the main dissecting room with about a dozen tanks in it. For some reason they've painted the walls bright orange and the ceiling silver. It's very quaint and you get a swell view from there. My office is in a tiny gable all of its own. You get to it from one corner of the dissecting room by a spiral iron staircase. You must let me take you up there sometime. I think it would amuse you. They're not supposed to allow visitors, but I'm more or less in charge there three nights a week, Mondays, Wednesdays, and Fridays, just to see that they are all out by ten o'clock, and the lights are off and so on."

"But I should think it would be sort of spooky," she exclaimed, "up there at night! But of course if there are other people . . ."

"Good heavens no!" He laughed. "As I said, there's a sort of family atmosphere. But what I like best is after I've kicked out the students at ten o'clock. Then I almost always stay myself till midnight or after. It's completely quiet, and you feel so alone, it's wonderful for concentrating. You look down over fire escapes and all kinds of steep

55

slate roofs, and you can see little lights over the country here and there in houses miles away. That's when I get most of my own research done."

"I've noticed a light way up in the top of the building very late at night," she said. "Sometimes I've wondered what it was. I've always imagined it was something rather macabre and secret."

He laughed again with his usual gay abruptness. "Far from it," he said. "If it's macabre, it's only so for my poor little mice."

At first they had passed a number of canoes, but now that they had reached the middle of the lake they were alone except for two or three small sailboats, perhaps a quarter of a mile away, trying to make the best of what breeze they could catch. She looked over her shoulder at the far side of the lake, a wild shore partly wooded, partly low marshland, where she had never been.

"Where are we going?" she asked.

"Do you see that group of poplars, and the lone willow a hundred yards to the left of them? We go in beside that willow. It's a little creek that leads to some springs. And no matter how hot the sun gets you'll find that the water there is as cold as if it had been drawn from a well."

"That seems too good to be true!" she exclaimed, and as she glanced up at Dave, so neat and strong and brown, so considerate, so competent, she felt that that was the only trouble with him: he was too good to be true. There must be some flaw, some weakness beneath the surface, which she certainly could not guess and would probably never discover. She smiled at her line of reasoning and wondered what he would say if she told him what she was thinking. She was sure at any rate that he would not be in the least embarrassed.

As they approached the bushy shore they slipped by sheets of cow lilies, with worm-eaten oily-looking pads among which small white snail shells were floating; dragonflies darted over the water; the hum of insects grew louder. The creek was not more than ten feet wide, and so shallow that sometimes the canoe scraped on the mud and Dave had to use his paddle as a pole. It wound through thickets of

56

dogwood and osiers, past beds of reeds and tufts of early goldenrod. After the first few turns Daphne had no idea in what direction they were going, and whether they had been following the creek for a few hundred yards or perhaps for nearly a mile.

At last the water deepened suddenly, no longer slimy but clear now and green, the banks widened, and they came out into a pond with streams trickling from masses of bright green cress and sliding over stones in a series of miniature rapids. Dave drew up beside a tongue of short grass. They stepped out of the canoe, and pulled the bow up on to the bank.

Beyond the plot of grass and the water cress a dense wood shut off any distant view; the twisted roots, the pale trunks of half-fallen trees, made her think of some tropical bayou, or the shores of the Amazon.

"It's beautiful!" she exclaimed. "And how far away it seems! You can't imagine any other people for miles and miles."

"As a matter of fact," he said, "I doubt if there is any house within a good mile of here, and that wood is so marshy it's next to impossible to get here from the landward side. Now I'm going to forage for some wood, but you better not leave this grass, because the ground is treacherous in there and you're apt to step through up to your knees in mud unless you're very careful."

While Dave went off into the woods, Daphne knelt down upon the tufted bank, dipped her arms into the cold water, and splashed it over her face and neck. Although the little plot of grass was in full sunlight and the breeze did not penetrate the thickets, the air seemed cooled by the spring, and Daphne loved the smell of the marsh. A few yards from shore she could see small frogs clinging to stones, with just their heads out of water, their hind legs dragging in the current; and when she stood up and walked around a quantity of small violet butterflies kept rising from the grass and fluttering about her ankles. She felt happy and at peace; last night's experience might have occurred weeks ago.

When Dave returned with the wood he poured out cocktails from one of the thermos bottles, and she watched him break the dead branches into fagots and build the most symmetrical little fire she had ever seen. He was telling her about his work with mice; he had a grant from the university to experiment with hormones in relation to cancer. "But I ought to be finished this fall," he said. "I mean with the particular piece of work I'm doing now. Then I'm going to waive my deferment and get into the Army. The ski-troops, if I can. Of course nothing is sure about the Army, but I've got a bit of a pull and they're glad to get men who are really at home on skis. At least they were some time ago. I've heard rumors lately that they may disband them, but I hope not."

"But wouldn't you have to go into the Medical Corps?" she asked.

"I'm not an M.D.," he explained. "You knew that, didn't you? I'm just a Ph.D. in biology. There's nothing special about them. There are far fewer good skiers than there are biologists."

She smiled. "You *would* be going into the ski troops," she said. "That fits in perfectly with my picture of you."

He sent her a quick glance. "Could you give me some idea of what that picture is? Or perhaps I'd be happier not knowing."

"Not at all," she said. "It's the picture of a rather romantic young man . . . just the kind that would be in the ski troops, something quite active with a good deal of glamour." She smiled at him. "I could easily imagine you on a poster, skiing down a snowy mountainside, with JOIN THE SKI TROOPS printed above you in red, white, and blue lettering."

"I don't know that I like that," he said. "Posters are only cardboard."

She blushed faintly, because she remembered that when she saw him for the first time, at Terry's, she had thought of him precisely as a sort of cardboard young man.

They toasted wieners over the fire; he poured hot coffee from the other thermos bottle, and fried in the skillet a combination of onions, mushrooms, and green peppers.

"I see you're an excellent cook," she said. "It doesn't surprise me."

As he put the empty skillet behind him on the grass, a large frog jumped away and splashed into the pond.

"That reminds me," he said, "I was going to carve you a toad, wasn't I? How about a frog instead?"

"Do you do them from life?" she asked.

"They don't have to pose, but I like to have them around when I'm working, just to remind me how they fit together."

"I'd love to have a frog, and perhaps sometime you'll carve me a toad to keep him company."

"I'll say!" he exclaimed. "But you better wait until you see the frog first."

When they had finished their last cup of coffee and put away the picnic things, he drew a long clasp knife from his pocket, opened it carefully, felt the edge of the blade with his finger, and then whetted it several times on the sole of his moccasin.

"What a vicious-looking knife!" she said.

"It does its job. Between you and me, the blade is a little longer than I'd be allowed to carry by law, but I'll take the chance of being hauled up for toting concealed weapons. I'd feel lost without that knife. You see I put myself entirely at your mercy."

"Of course I shall go right to the police," she told him.

He ran his finger once more along the blade, smiling to himself. "You've forgotten," he said, "that you have to get home first."

Just then through the woods behind them there came the sound of boys' voices. Daphne was sorry to hear them, because it seemed to break the spell, to jerk them back from this peaceful out-of-doors world into the midst of people. Dave swore so low under his breath that she could not distinguish what he said; then he looked at her with such a woeful expression that she knew he must feel much as she did at the interruption.

"Wouldn't you know it!" he exclaimed. "I chose this place because I thought it was the one bit of shore where we would be left alone."

"They'll probably be moving on, won't they?"

"Don't you believe it. They've come to catch frogs. I used to do it myself when I was a boy."

Two boys about twelve years old stepped out from between the trees; they were barefoot and carried their shoes in their hands. They tactfully went twenty yards or so down the creek, but you could still see them through the reeds and hear their voices. She watched Dave as he carved with remarkable swiftness a slender squatting frog from a bit of dried wood, but she thought he had lost some of his gaiety. By midafternoon she suggested their starting back.

The morning's breeze had died. As he paddled back across the lake, Dave spoke very little. Daphne watched the town float nearer and nearer—the men's gymnasium, the top of the hotel on the square, the fraternity houses, the red gabled mass of Science Hall. By the time they were halfway across she could make out her own apartment behind its hickory tree. Windows in the buildings along shore gleamed through the warm haze, and smoke from the few factory chimneys rose straight into the whitish sky.

They were passing now between numbers of other canoes. Daphne did not know whether it was because of Dave's change of mood, but she found herself feeling more and more depressed: the elation of the day was gone. The springs in the water cress, the small blue butterflies, the smell of the swamp, they all seemed as far away as the town had seemed a little while ago. She could hardly bear to set foot on shore, to be trapped once again among the hot airless houses and the people, trapped like Margaret Peterson and that poor dead girl whose body had been found, covered with flies, among the wilted brambles.

As Dave was escorting her along College Street to her rooms, they overtook Edwin Voigt. If she could hear him play tonight, that might be the one thing that would make her happy again, but she knew he was very fussy about playing, and only liked to when he felt in the mood.

"How beautifully sunburned you both look!" he said. "Have you been on the lake?"

"We've been across it," she told him; "to a most perfect spot. We've been out all day."

"I envy you," Edwin said. "I'd like to get away from this damn town for a few days. No one seems to talk about anything except the murders. I think it's nauseating."

"There was only one murder," Dave said.

"Well, the murder then," he said pettishly. "Just because we were at Terry's that night and came home through the woods, they seem to think we must be authorities on the subject. At least I don't know about you, but that's been my experience. I don't know how many people have asked me if I actually heard the scream."

"Did you?" Dave asked.

"Of course I didn't," Edwin snapped. "Thank God!"

After Edwin had left them, a moment later, to go into the Union, Daphne felt uncomfortably that perhaps her insistence to Harold that he shouldn't talk about the crimes, that he shouldn't have anything to do with them, might have sounded to him as finicky and squeamish as Edwin had just sounded to her.

Before her apartment she held out her hand to Dave. "I can't thank you enough," she said. "I simply loved it."

He held her hand for an instant. "It was the happiest day of my life," he said. She felt rather guilty that his remark should have pleased her so much, and as soon as she entered the living room she called up Harold.

"Won't you come to supper?" she asked. "And darling, I want to tell you that you can go ahead with your investigation, as far as I'm concerned. In fact, I think I can make a small contribution myself."

CHAPTER VIII

*W*HEN Harold put down the telephone, he was almost frightened by his sense of relief. It was as if a window which had been closed since yesterday morning, shutting him into a room where he could hardly breathe, had suddenly again been flung open, and all the air from the cool upper spaces of the sky had rushed in to soothe and refresh him, to bring him back to life. It was extraordinary how he had come to depend on Daphne. "Certainly for me," he thought, remembering the line of Baudelaire, "she is *l'Ange gardien, la Muse et la Madone.*"

This was truer than ever now that he was drenched in the

atmosphere of these crimes. Surely the mysterious attacker could not be found by conventional police methods; and yet it might be just as futile to dream of the man himself, to try to materialize him by the sheer force of imagination and construct a recognizable image of the criminal by brooding over every aspect of the crime. When you got too close to something, when it became too exciting, too much a part of you, it grew difficult to separate what you had observed from what your fantasy had created. That cocktail napkin, for example. . . . But no, he was sure there. His reasoning was quite objective: that alone cut down the field of possibilities, so enormously that it was worth all his efforts, his fatigue, and his concentration. That was the one real clue, and it was he, not the police, who had found it.

He stripped off his clothes excitedly and took a cold shower. The tiny white bathroom looked cooler and more cheerful than his combined study and bedroom. At first he had been fond of this room, delighted to have collected all his books and put them in order at last; but recently it had seemed to him cluttered and depressing. Book-lined walls were interesting and decorative, but in this hot weather they seemed to absorb half the air and light; and if you let yourself start thinking of the separate volumes, which sometimes was hard to prevent when you sat too long alone, it made concentration difficult.

When he left his rooming house, he still felt nicely cooled by his shower, but he hurried so on his way to Daphne's apartment that by the time he had climbed her stairs and stood before her door, the fresh shirt he had just put on was sticking to his back. The morning had been so breezy that he had hoped tonight would be cool, but it seemed to him now that this was one of the warmest evenings of the summer. When Daphne opened the door, he stepped eagerly in and took her into his arms.

"Before you say anything else," he exclaimed, with a twinge of anxiety in the midst of his very happiness, "you must promise me that you'll never quarrel with me again. I may often be doing things you don't like, but then you must punish me at once and get it over with. You've no idea how miserable I've been, Daphne."

62

"I hated it too," she said. "But I've been so on edge this last week . . ."

"Of course I don't blame you," he said quickly. "So have I. And I could see how it must have seemed callous and deceitful my going to the police and all that. As a matter of fact, they have been very pleasant, but I don't think they have taken my efforts seriously. I'll tell you about that later, if you'd like to hear it. But what you didn't understand, darling, is the way these crimes have been pursuing me. I've always been interested in such things, Daphne, you know that. I've always been fascinated by the strange twists of the mind. That's why I went into psychology in the first place: to try to understand other people, even the strangest, and myself most of all. I just couldn't keep my hands out of this business, Daphne. I was interested enough in the first one, the real murder; but then this second one, the attempt, and my being right there, getting my fingers right into it . . . it seemed almost like fate!"

He stopped short and laughed. "Of course that's ridiculous. I shudder to think of what my colleagues would say, if they heard me using such an expression. It's just that I feel so excited to be with you again that I can't stop talking."

He looked happily around the bright living room. Through the open window he could see a strip of the lake, dark blue beneath the slanting sunlight. The glowing white curtains suggested the softest clouds or the feathers of birds; the painted tulips above the mantelpiece had the mystery, the intensity of living flowers. No other place had ever seemed to him so cheerful, so secure.

"I feel the way Adam would have felt," he exclaimed, "if he had been given a second chance at Eden."

She smiled at him affectionately. "You make *me* feel very guilty," she said. "And now you can mix us a drink. Whatever you like. You know what's in the house. And when we're drinking it, I must tell you about my experience. While you've been after the murderer, Harold darling, I very much suspect that he's been after me."

"What do you mean?" he asked. "You must be mistaken, dearest. You must have been imagining."

63

He was shocked and incredulous; and yet on second thoughts if this were Eden what would be more natural than that Satan should seek an entrance?

While he made a couple of Tom Collinses, Daphne told him of her midnight visitor. Then she took him on to the balcony outside her bedroom window and he saw for himself the torn bark, the broken twigs. It was particularly exciting to discover these traces of the murderer now that he had made his own discovery.

"But you can't be sleeping here after this," he said. "How do you know he won't come back?"

"I'm going to sleep across the hall with Gerty and Mary," she said.

"Of course I think it's unlikely that he'll try this again, once you've scared him off. He probably won't dare, unless the urge becomes irresistible. Then he might risk anything. But you poor little thing, you must have been terrified!"

He put his arm around her rather guiltily, because he realized that for the first moment he had not been thinking of her but of the murderer. The urge must have been strong indeed to force him to climb this tree, a difficult task even without the risk of discovery, for the lower branches were far apart and looked none too convenient.

"Until yesterday," he said, "I'd have suggested your moving out to the Macfarlanes'. Jeanne I know would have been delighted to have you, but as it is, I think it's just as well for you to move in with Gerty McNeill."

"What do you mean?" she asked. "What happened yesterday?"

He rubbed his hands and walked up and down the living room, occasionally stopping to sip his drink which he had placed on the mantelpiece.

"Ah, that's my news," he exclaimed. "I've been crazy to tell you all day, but I didn't dare until you gave me some sign. I felt that you had pushed me into the outer darkness, dearest; but perhaps in the long run it may have been as well, because it was while working in the darkness, all alone, that I made my discovery."

"But what did you discover?"

He gave her a long look, smiling to himself at her curiosity. He noticed how brown she was, how much a creature of wind and sun: no one could possibly seem more remote from the world of these crimes, and yet last night proved that perhaps as she had feared, the murderer had fixed his mind upon her. "It's lucky I'm here," he thought. "If I depend on her for my happiness, this makes her now also depend on me . . . perhaps for her very life."

"But what is it?" she asked again. "Tell me, Harold. Do you think it's important?"

He realized that he had been staring at her without speaking for almost a minute.

"Important!" he exclaimed. "I should say so! It has narrowed the murderer down to a handful of people. Do you remember that evening of the dinner, I said he might be any one of us there at table? In a way that was prophetic, because now I know, I'm personally convinced, though the police won't grant as much, that it must have been one of those men. That's why I wouldn't want you to stay now at Terry's. How ironical if you should seek refuge perhaps in the murderer's own house!"

She looked at him in such amazement that he felt a warm thrill of triumph. "But Harold, you surely don't believe for a moment that Terry . . ."

"No, as a matter of fact, I don't," he said. "I'd be very much surprised if it were he, though as far as time and distance are concerned it wouldn't be impossible. When the woman called him that night, it was Jeanne who answered. Jeanne told me so herself. Terry was walking around the place, she says. She called him but he didn't show up for perhaps ten minutes. He could have run that distance, less than a mile, without too much difficulty. You remember, he didn't reach the scene of the attack until quite a while after the police got there. However, as I said, it would have had to be such a close shave that it would have been all but impossible; and besides from what I know of Terry I'd have been inclined to rank him as the least likely in any case."

"Terry couldn't have been following me on the way out," she said.

"That's true, of course. It's just one more reason for discarding him, though we can't assume absolutely that that

65

was the same man. Still, I think we can forget Terry for the time being."

"But do tell me what it was," she urged. "You're sure it's not just your theory, Harold . . . some psychological theory?"

"It's good solid fact," he said. "Listen, Daphne. Yesterday morning, after our quarrel, I went out again to the woods. I'd been there several times before. I'd talked the whole thing over with the police. I'd tried to make them see that their idea of a tramp or a roughneck was all wrong; but although they were polite enough I could see they put me down as just another of those crazy professors. The trouble is I'd let myself get too excited when I was talking with them. I should have made a point of keeping calm. Well, to go back to yesterday morning: you'd made me feel so discouraged, that I thought I'd start all over again from the beginning. You were angry with me for going to the police, and yet it had done no good. I felt that I simply would have to justify it. So I searched the leaves and the brambles for yards around, not looking for anything especial, feeling that I was doing exactly what I'd said from the start would be quite futile, but at last, in the ditch at the edge of the road, about twenty yards from where the girl was lying, I found what for a moment I took for a rumpled handkerchief. It was so small I thought it must be hers; but when I spread it out I saw it was a cocktail napkin, one of those with the little embroidered cock and the initials J.M. underneath it, exactly like the ones we'd had at Terry's that evening. It was all draggled and clotted up with dried mud, almost entirely hidden by some nettles. I'd never have seen it if I hadn't been prying among the weeds by the road. The police had done it too, but very superficially, and they hadn't gone so far away."

He looked at her closely to discover how his news had affected her, but she still seemed merely puzzled.

"But how could a cocktail napkin get there?" she asked. "If it had been a handkerchief, I could understand . . ."

"But don't you see," he went on eagerly, "someone slipped the napkin into his pocket absent-mindedly, as if it were a handkerchief. Quite often I've found napkins in the pockets of my dinner clothes and have no idea where I picked them up. I'm sure a great many men do. After I'd found the napkin I examined the underbrush very carefully and although I couldn't be sure, it looked as if it might have been very near that spot where he sprang out on her. Perhaps when he pulled the knife from his pocket the napkin came with it, or perhaps it only came partly out and was jerked or shaken the rest of the way when they struggled, before she broke away from him and started to run. Now, Daphne, tell me, what do you think of that?"

"I hardly know what to think," she said, and he saw that at last his news had struck home: she had grown pale beneath her tan; her eyes were strained and frightened, and he even suspected that for an instant she had felt faint. "It seems to me utterly impossible that any of those men . . ."

"But that's just the point!" he exclaimed excitedly. "It's not impossible for anyone. You remember I stressed that too."

"But Harold, have you told the police? What do they think?"

"You must remember," he said, "that they are ignorant men. They are not used to this kind of thing. They admitted that there might possibly be something in what I said. They are even going so far as to question all four men— Terry, Edwin, Dave, and Paul; but they said that I might have dropped the napkin myself. They examined it for fingerprints but it had been so thoroughly drenched by the thunderstorm and caked with dirt they couldn't get anything. Unfortunately I told them, just as I told you a minute ago, that I sometimes had stuffed them into my own pocket, and they jumped on that at once. Or they suggested that Terry might have. I'm just as glad in a way that they weren't more impressed, because they promised they would not speak to anyone until I'd interviewed them myself. A clumsy police interview would be enough to put the man on his guard; and now that you have told me I can go ahead, with your full approval. . . ."

"But why mightn't you have dropped it, Harold, you or Terry?"

"For the simple reason that I'm sure I never went as far back along the road, and I'm sure Terry didn't either. He came in his car, of course, and stopped not ten feet from where the girl was lying. The police seem to think it's impossible to tell exactly where anyone was, on account of the excitement and confusion. But I know. I tell you I know."

"But Harold, it couldn't have been Dave any more than Terry. Why, the idea is ridiculous. I can't even think that you believe it."

"After all," he said, "Dave walked home alone through the woods, not so long after we did. He admitted as much to you himself."

"Admitted it!" she exclaimed, and he noticed with a queer uneasy feeling that she sounded indignant. "You talk as if there were anything wrong with it. He told me so, yes, but I certainly didn't think that when I mentioned it to you . . ."

"Don't get excited, dearest," he said. "I know you like Dave," and he prided himself on the detachment in his voice. "If it's any consolation to you, I think there is almost as little chance of his being the one as Terry."

He noticed her relief, and the strange feeling inside him crystallized into a sharp and momentary jealousy: of all the four he would rather that it be Dave; because Dave was the youngest, the handsomest, because Dave had been seeing Daphne at every opportunity; but he felt it was a credit to his detachment, his perfect fairness, that he never had really considered Dave except in the most perfunctory way. Still, there might be danger here: knowing that he had a grudge against Dave, he must take care that his sense of justice did not make him lean over backwards and assume his innocence simply because he had a reason for wishing him guilty.

"If I don't suspect Dave," he could not resist adding, "it's just because he impresses me as an utterly normal and commonplace young man."

"As a matter of fact," she said quickly, "both Edwin and Mr. Hatfield walked through the wood alone on their way home that evening. Mr. Hatfield happened to mention it the day I lunched with him downtown."

68

"Yes, I found that out too," Harold said. "Wanda told me. I take it you would rather have it either Edwin or Paul than Dave? Am I right?"

"I certainly couldn't bear for it to be Dave," she said earnestly, "but I don't want it to be one of them either. It's almost as hard to believe. . . . I simply can't believe it, Harold. The idea makes me feel actually sick . . . or perhaps it's just the strain of trying to make it seem possible."

"Listen," he said, "I know how you feel, darling, but I certainly must go ahead now. Supposing that last night the man, whoever he was, hadn't waked you up until he had got into your room . . ."

"Don't!" she exclaimed with a half sob. "Oh Harold, please don't!"

He went to her quickly and put his hand on her shoulder.

"I'm sorry," he said, "I only want to show you how important it is to trap the murderer. And if you're thinking of Terry . . . or Dave, I don't think you need be disturbed. It's either Paul or Edwin, I'm nearly sure of it. I've thought of each one of them, each of the four, as a possible case, and as I said, neither Dave nor Terry fits at all, unless I've completely misunderstood them. Of course that's not impossible. We should always bear that in mind."

"If you think that Dave is commonplace . . ." she began.

"It may be lucky for him he is," Harold said brusquely. "But Edwin and Paul—they are quite a different story. They are both complicated and interesting people. They are both in a measure thwarted. Paul is ignored by Wanda. He must once have been in love with her, but now to all intents he is unattached, and quite possibly has a grievance against all women. He's at a dangerous age. He has always been interested in crime, in abnormality of every description. He's thoroughly acquainted with the history of every mass murderer that anyone knows anything about. He's been fascinated by the subject, and one can't overemphasize —as I was saying at Terry's—how insidious and powerful the force of suggestion is. There's a certain queerness inside Paul that I've never entirely understood. Nothing that I discovered about him would really surprise me very much."

"But he seems to be such a kind man," Daphne protested.

69

Harold shrugged his shoulders: he must not let himself feel that Daphne was attacking him. "But darling, haven't I told you that whether the man is kind or gentle or affectionate has not the slightest bearing on the case? Unless you might say that a sadist was more apt to be softhearted. The more violence he does to his own nature, the more kindly he feels toward his victim, the greater must be the intensity of the emotional experience."

"How horrible!" Daphne exclaimed.

"We're moving in a region of horror," Harold said "—at least what appears horror to the average mind. But let's take Edwin: he is certainly far from the average. He's a very solitary young man, slightly effeminate. So far as I know he's never had even a passing flirtation with a young woman. You can see from his music that he's far more emotional than you'd ever guess from his manner. In fact you might easily imagine that he deliberately cultivated his manner to hide his emotions. You've spoken once or twice to me jokingly about his mustache. I remember your saying it seemed sometimes as if he were hiding behind it. I think that may be quite true. And what has he been hiding? Perhaps the urge to kill that he struggled against for who knows how long until at last, one day, it got the better of him. That's what I must do next, Daphne; I must do it right off: I must talk to Edwin and Paul . . . the others, yes, but to Paul and Edwin first. They can't suspect that I have any reason to believe they are associated with the crimes. Perhaps, if I'm lucky, one or the other may give himself away . . . not actually, I mean, but just to me, so that I at least will be sure. That will be a great deal accomplished. But then to convict him. . . . Ah, that's a different question. Perhaps we may simply have to wait, to wait and to watch. . . . But look here, I mustn't talk like this forever. We must be getting supper. What do you want me to do? Shall I set the table, darling?"

Suddenly her shoulder trembled violently beneath his fingers and she flung her head forward into her hands.

"I don't care," she exclaimed. "I can't eat now. I can't think. It's all too dreadful!"

"But darling—" he bent over her anxiously; he did his
70

best to sooth her "—for your own sake, you ought to know what I suspect. You're not angry with me again, are you?"

"No, no," she sobbed, "I'm not angry. It's not your fault. But I'm scared. I'm tired. It's all been such an awful nightmare, this whole last week. If it keeps on much longer, I feel that I'll go crazy myself."

"Daphne, dearest!" He knelt down in front of her and put his hands to hers as if to uncover her face. "Daphne, look at me. You're the sanest person I know. You're everything that's sane and lovely and unspoiled. I'm the crazy one to be tormenting you like this. But listen, Daphne. Why won't you marry me, after all? There is no real reason for putting it off any longer. Then you'd never be alone again, and neither would I. You've no idea how I hate it! Would you, Daphne? So much might depend on it—for both of us!"

His heart had begun to pound violently; her hands yielded to his, and again, in the hot twilight, he could see her face looking down at him through her tears. She might be leaning, like the Blessed Damozel, over the balcony of heaven. He stared intensely, eagerly into her eyes to try to make out what she was thinking, what she was feeling. It seemed to him that his eternal destiny depended on her answer.

At last she shook her head and made an effort to smile.

"No," she said, "I can't quite yet, Harold. It still seems strange to me. I still don't feel quite ready. I still feel so lonely and confused after Mother's death. You don't mind waiting a little longer, do you, Harold? You'd certainly want me to be absolutely sure. You said you understood."

"Yes, yes, I do," he exclaimed quickly. "But it's different now. You need me to protect you, Daphne. It's a question . . . it may be a question of life or death . . ."

He watched her tensely, but already he knew that there was no use: it was like the dimming of a light, the fading of music.

"You wouldn't want me to be scared into marrying you, would you?" she asked, and her smile seemed so pathetic, so childlike, that it brought tears into his own eyes—tears as much for her as for himself. "But Harold, I'll count on

71

you just as much. even if we're not married. Because you have no idea how scared I am. I'm really scared underneath, every minute of the time. And now. while you've been talking and while it's been growing dark, and the air feels so thick and dead, I'm just beginning to remember how terrified I was last night, like a fly caught in a web as it waits for the spider's coming. And I don't see how it can end. It will just go on and on. It will get worse and worse . . ."

"There *will* be an end," he said, "I promise you. And then everything will be all right again. The bad dream will be over—the dream of darkness and blood—and we can both forget about it. Perhaps—who knows?—the end will come sooner than we think."

CHAPTER IX

THE next afternoon Harold called on the Hatfields. As he waited on their steps in the sun, he was considering whether he should let Paul know about the cocktail napkin. If he were guilty it would of course put him on his guard; and yet his learning so suddenly that he was under suspicion might tend to make him reveal his guilt in the first moment of his surprise and fear.

Harold wiped his forehead and his neck inside his damp open collar. It was hard to think clearly in this persistent heat. His head was ringing with the chirp of crickets and cicadas. The tall junipers in the garden might have been obelisks of hot green bronze; their shadows ate into the ground like sweeps of transparent ink, and Harold was reminded of pictures he had seen of gardens in Persia or India, the gardens of princes, kept green by constant irrigation in the midst of dessicated and sweltering cities.

He looked down at the clumps of blazing salmon-colored phlox beside the steps and noticed stretched between two stems the web of a ladder spider. The large spider itself hung motionless, with jet-black legs and yellow tiger-striped body, as brilliant as any of the flowers. He recalled how Daphne had said last night that she felt like a fly caught in a web; and it occurred to him that if Paul were warned,

72

if he knew that Harold had his eye on him, that would certainly tend to keep him away from Daphne. It would be a move toward her protection; but how could Paul be finally convicted?

Harold realized that this was where his thoughts had started a few moments ago: in this iridescent glare they were moving in circles. The door was opening. It would be easier to make up his mind in the coolness of the house.

It was Wanda who let him in. She wore cherry-colored slacks and a sea-green blouse. He could see fine drops of sweat beneath the powder on her cheeks and forehead.

"Hullo, stranger!" she said. "This is marvelous. I've just been lying on the hammock on the back porch trying to get up enough energy to make myself a long cool drink; and now you have done the trick. Come in! We'll go right into the kitchen."

"Is Paul here?" he asked as he followed her out through the pantry.

"Now don't tell me you came to see him!" she exclaimed. "And I was just flattering myself that I'd lured you away from Daphne, if only for half an hour."

"I came to see both of you," he said with a smile.

"Well, Paul should be back at any time. At least I suppose he will be. He never tells me of his comings and goings. Now, my dear, if you'd get some ice cubes over there. I'm not going to make anything fancy. It's too hot. Just plain bourbon and water."

If Harold regretted Wanda's presence, he was thankful for the prospect of a cool drink. He piled up the ice in a bowl Wanda passed him, and in a few moments she led him through the big living room, dim with lowered shades, on to the screened-in porch that looked toward the lake across a lawn and a small formal garden. He was glad to see that she had brought along the bottle and a pitcher of water.

Wanda stretched herself in the hammock and he sat down on a small metal chair beside her.

"It may be hotter out here," she said. "God knows! But looking at the lake and the boats makes it seem cooler—at least that's my theory. Did Daphne have a good time yesterday?"

73

"Yesterday?" he repeated. He tried to think of what Daphne had been doing and remembered that he had not seen her until the evening.

"Don't tell me I've put my foot in it!" Wanda exclaimed. "I supposed of course you knew all about it!"

"About what?" he asked uneasily.

"Nothing," she said, and he could see that she was enjoying herself. "You have no right to bawl her out, Harold. After all, the girl's of age, and Dave is most attractive—that is if you like the sexy type."

"Dave?" He was still puzzled. "Of course I know that Dave's a friend of hers."

Wanda slowly smiled. "It's so sensible to be broad-minded," she said with an exaggeration of her usual drawl. "After all, a man can't keep his fiancée locked up the way they used to do, or his wife either, for that matter. We have passed the age of chastity belts. And my theory is that a girl who looks around a bit is apt to settle down eventually into the best kind of wife. Just look at me, for instance—sitting here twirling my thumbs until Paul comes home, ready to greet him with a dutiful smile and a long cool drink."

"I wish you'd tell me what you're driving at," Harold said. He knew that anything Wanda said would be because she was jealous; he knew the wise thing would be to give her no satisfaction; but his tormented curiosity would not leave him in peace.

"Yesterday morning I was cutting flowers in the garden," she said, "just like a Victorian heroine, and I saw Daphne and Dave setting out across the lake. I must say they make a very handsome couple. I was faintly curious to see when they'd come back. I suppose I really felt sort of responsible, being such an old friend of yours, though after all, what could I do? What can anyone do in a case like that? And of course I assumed she had told you. If I hadn't, wild horses couldn't have dragged the secret from me. Well, my dear, I thought I must have missed them, because naturally I didn't keep my eyes glued to the lake all day; but not at all. Some time in the late afternoon they passed by again. I thought Daphne looked rather tired, but that's what you'd expect. It's a long way across there, and you remember how hot it grew by afternoon. It was a very enervating day."

Harold forced himself to grin. "You do it very well, Wanda darling," he said. "The wealth of suggestion you put into the one word 'enervating' wouldn't have passed the Hays office, if this had been a scene in a movie, which it might very well have been. But Daphne is quite free to picnic with whom she pleases. It would no more occur to me to be jealous of her canoeing with Dave than it would to her to be jealous of my having a drink with you—as I am just now, and thoroughly enjoying it, by the way."

"If you're enjoying yourself, that's all I could ask," she said, and patted his knee. "You're a sweet boy, Harold. You may read Freud all day and the Marquis de Sade all night, but you have kept your original innocence, and I hope to God you always do. I love you that way. But you've finished your drink. Pour yourself another, and we'll only hope that Paul doesn't come barging in too soon."

While Harold poured out his second highball, he kept repeating to himself that it was an insult to Daphne for him to be jealous because she had picnicked with Dave. It wasn't merely the fact that she had gone, of course: it was her not mentioning it last evening. When he had suggested that Dave was among the immediate suspects she must at once have thought of their trip across the lake. This was surely the explanation of her sudden horror at the idea of his possible guilt.

He took a long swallow of the drink he had just poured out: he must be terribly overwrought if he allowed anything Wanda could say to come even for a moment between Daphne and him. Yet now across the scorched lawn and the bright squares of flowers, he caught himself squinting at the canoes he could see passing over the oil-smooth water, as if perhaps in one of them, leaning back among cushions and staring in admiration at a dark lithe torso, a bold and handsome face, he might discover Daphne.

"Why hullo, Harold! This is a pleasant surprise."

Harold turned in relief to the door into the living room: Paul stood on the threshold in a rumpled coffee-colored suit. His hair looked dusty; he wore sandals and no socks.

75

"I hope this means you'll stay for dinner," he went on. "I haven't had a real chance to talk with you since that night at Terry's. You were the lucky one, weren't you, to be so near the scene of the crime. I did have a nice little chat with Daphne a few days ago. She probably told you."

Paul stepped to the table and poured himself a drink in the extra glass that Wanda had placed on the tray. Was this bluff, Harold wondered, this almost headlong reference to the attack? Paul's hand was completely steady as he poured the whisky; his face kept the carved, wooden look which it wore most of the time. At any rate he must accept the invitation, Harold decided: he must not lose the chance that Paul had offered him.

"I'd love to stay," he said, "if it's all right with Wanda."

"I think it would be just perfect," she exclaimed. "I'd suggest having Daphne too, but I'm sure she'll be able to look out for herself."

"I'm sure she will," Harold said. "In fact I happen to know that she is having dinner with Mary Sharpe and Gertrude McNeill."

Wanda smiled as she pulled herself up from her hammock.

"So she is having supper with Mary and Gertrude! That sounds harmless. Well, we girls must stick together, mustn't we? And now, being thoroughly domestic, I'm going into the kitchen and make you boys a little curry. I hope you like things hot, Harold?"

"She mustn't do anything special," Harold exclaimed as Wanda moved languidly through the doorway.

"Oh, don't worry about that," Paul said. "Wanda really loves to cook, especially the more exotic dishes, and I'm afraid I'm apt to be unappreciative because I like nothing so much myself as canned corn beef hash and tomato ketchup. Of course nowadays even that is quite a luxury. Poor Wanda has certain talents and certain virtues. As a rule they bear little relation to each other; but her cooking is the one case in which they coincide. Since Hildegard left to go into a munitions factory we haven't been able to find another maid, at least at a price we can afford, and Wanda has done nobly. I'd be the first to admit it."

Harold leaned forward, staring at Paul. He realized that it was perhaps because he had drunk two highballs, perhaps because Wanda's talk had excited and disturbed him, but nonetheless he had suddenly made up his mind that he must plunge forward. He would break the news to Paul at once and then see what happened.

"Paul," he began abruptly, "you were speaking of the attack just now. I know that it was made by someone who had dined at Terry's that evening."

Paul did not start; he did not show any surprise. His pale birdlike eyes merely stared back at Harold.

"Dear me!" he exclaimed gently, "that's interesting. But may I ask how you can be so sure?"

"I found a crumpled cocktail napkin, the kind we had that evening, by the side of the road—only a few yards from where the man left the bushes."

Paul stroked his chin. "I see," he murmured. "And you assume it was dropped by the murderer—for I'm taking it for granted that it was the same man. Of course, Harold, I hate to throw cold water on your theory, but had it occurred to you that it might have been dropped there previously? After all, the Macfarlanes entertain quite frequently, and that bit of road is almost on a direct line between their house and town, if you go by the woods. Of course not quite: I admit that."

"It did occur to me," Harold said, "but it seemed to me that that would be too much of a coincidence." Did it mean anything, he wondered, that Paul seemed eager to deny the importance of this clue?

"Yes, I agree with you. It would. I've no doubt you have something there. Dear, dear, that makes us all suspects, doesn't it?" He smiled for an instant, and Harold felt that he found the idea rather pleasant.

"Yes," Harold said. "All except me."

"You too," Paul corrected him, "although rather a remote one. Of course you could use Daphne as an alibi, but what's to prevent her being a party to the crime, an interested onlooker, so to speak? I've never heard of a mass murderer accomplishing his killings in his fiancée's presence—with the possible exception of Burke, and that term would

77

hardly apply to Helen M'Dougal—but it would make an interesting variation. You understand," he said with a deprecatory air, "I'm not for an instant casting any reflections upon Daphne. I think she's a sweet lovely girl. I'm speaking from the point of view of the pure theorist. No, I admit I'd be surprised if you were the one this time."

"His voice," Harold thought, "sounded almost regretful." Suddenly Paul smiled again, as if something at once amusing and agreeable had entered his mind.

"I suppose you came here this evening because you thought I might be he," he said. "Well, well, one never knows what may turn up. I certainly never thought I'd be a leading suspect for mass murder."

Harold gave a short laugh. "It's hardly mass murder yet," he said.

"Not yet, of course. You're quite right. But it may very well turn into that. Naturally I hope it won't; but if there were to be a series of murders, I mean a really distinguished one, one that would become a classic, like Burke and Hare, for example, it would be interesting for it to happen around here. Edinburgh is a famous place, rich in associations, but Burke and Hare and the dozen or more bodies they managed to dispose of to Dr. Knox—I think it was sixteen altogether, though I may be one or two off—have added a certain dingy luster to its legend. If Hanover should be destroyed in this war you can imagine some future student searching among the ruins for the site of Haarman's butcher shop where for all we know he may have sold to his customers the more succulent portions of his victims. Landru has added an aura of rather macabre poetry and surmise to the commonplace little French village of Gambais. One still wonders whether the bones of his various mistresses were entirely consumed in the stove inside his little rented villa. Yes, it would give a real distinction to Woodside to harbor a murderer in the grand manner, but my dear Harold, that's a distinction which will never devolve upon me personally. I'm immensely interested in the crimes, all the more so after what you have just told me, but—fortunately or unfortunately—I'm not the criminal."

"Whom would you suggest?" Harold asked. "You say it's

78 .

certainly not yourself and it's almost certainly not I."

"That leaves merely Terry, Dave Fulton, and Edwin Voigt, doesn't it? I'm not considering the women, although of course there have been women who committed murders of this sort—to mention only the notorious Countess Bathory, the Hungarian; but so far as I know their victims have always been men. One thing did occur to me on that evening. When you said that Terry's being a doctor would tend to disqualify him, you probably didn't recall that of the three suspects singled out by the police in the case of Jack the Ripper, two were doctors."

"I did remember that," Harold admitted, "after I'd said he might be a pre-Raphaelite painter, and of course he still might be: nothing was ever proved. But neither of those doctors was successful. One was a Russian of the most dubious reputation and the other was half mad and finally drowned himself in the Thames. But of course you know all about them—probably more than I do."

"There have been a great many doctors addicted to murder," Paul said thoughtfully. "Neil Cream, Crippen, De la Pommerais, not to mention Dr. William Palmer who killed, let me see . . . you don't happen to remember, do you? Of course there were his four legitimate and three illegitimate children, his wife, his mother-in-law, his own mother, his uncle, and a fair number of his friends. But it is true, as you brought out in the case of the Ripper suspects, these men were none of them really successful in their careers, at least in their medical careers. No, I'd be inclined to discount Terry, and I take it you have already done so."

Harold stared into the bottom of his empty glass: his mind felt for the moment just as empty—languidly ready to accept any suggestion. He was inclined to feel that Paul was telling the truth about himself; perhaps he would feel the same with Edwin; and then he would be just where he had started. Perhaps it was even true, as Paul had suggested, that the napkin was not associated with the attacker.

"Let me fill yours, won't you?" Paul suggested solicitously.

Harold reached him his glass. The garden was in shadow, but beyond the dark willows the surface of the lake was as luminous as the blue burnished wing of a butterfly. He could hear the voices of students in their boats so clearly that it seemed odd he could not distinguish any words. Nighthawks above the lake were dropping out of the blue and catching themselves in the strange game they liked to play. He remembered he had noticed one or two as he walked up Terry's drive that evening, already faintly worried about Daphne. It was hard to realize that that was only ten days ago.

He became aware that Paul was speaking again: "That would leave us Dave Fulton and Edwin Voigt, wouldn't it? Between Edwin and Dave, my bet would be Edwin every time, and I've no doubt yours would be, too, for very much the same reasons. Though looking at the whole thing objectively, as you must be doing, or at any rate trying to do, I can see that I would be a very likely suspect myself."

He poured himself another drink and glanced down at Harold, his head cocked perkily.

"It's fortunate it's not I," he said with his parrotlike chuckle, "because if it were, I think I could guarantee that the murderer would never be caught."

CHAPTER X

WHEN Harold left the Hatfields it was half-past ten o'clock. They had had more drinks after dinner. His head felt dizzy; his thoughts were swirling with a fatiguing restlessness, a kind of mechanical and strained expectation that seemed to have no object. Of course this was because he had drunk and smoked too much: since arriving at Paul's he had finished nearly two packs of cigarettes. As he walked along College Street beneath the dense branches of the maples, he thought of stopping in at Daphne's apartment to say good night, but she might have gone to bed, and he was afraid besides that he would show how much he had been drinking. He knew that his speech would be overdeliberate; that his eyes would have an unnatural glaze.

He stopped nonetheless for a minute in front of Daphne's apartment. He could not bear to go home; he knew that he could not sleep. that he could not even read just now: he would simply pace up and down in the heat, perhaps for hours. Then the impulse seized him to walk around to the back of the building and look up at Daphne's window as the murderer had done, from the foot of the hickory tree.

For no reason he gave a swift glance up and down the street to see that no one was coming, and then stepped quietly along the cement path into the shaded back yard. The lake was silent now. The hickory branches drooped thinly over him, and between their large clustered leaves he could see stars.

Directly above him, perhaps fifteen feet from the ground was the little balcony outside Daphne's bedroom. The window was dark tonight; that meant she was in bed—or no, she was not sleeping in this room, and even if she were he would see no light because the blinds would be drawn. He stood close against the tree and raised his arms to feel for the lowest branch. He could barely grasp it without standing on tiptoe, though with agility one could pull oneself up. It would be hard, though, for a man as old as Paul. Edwin was a little shorter than he was himself, but Edwin by an effort could probably manage it. The risk would be that someone would hear the rustling as Daphne had done, would look out and discover you, because the branches were not thick enough to give much concealment.

How excited the man must have been, how driven beyond himself to take that risk! Perhaps he had walked up and down in the street, careful not to be seen lingering near the building, debating, wondering, until at last he could resist no longer—until the urge for peace, for sleep, for a final and desperate consummation had pushed him on inevitably, no more able to resist than the moon could stop its own rising. Perhaps the incessant dry chirping of the crickets had formed itself into words in his ears, words meant only for him, which combined and became one with the words that the throbbing of his own blood kept whispering day and night, privately, voluptuously, deep in the center of his brain. It would not be hard then to climb this tree.

Then when the blinds had closed in his face, what a shock, what a dreadful awakening! And this for the second time!

81

How long could his racked mind, his whole tortured organism, endure these repeated frustrations?

Would it be Daphne whom he would seek again? Harold recalled how he had dismissed this idea when she had suggested it herself; but that had been partly to comfort her. After all, it was Daphne who had been followed through the wood; and now this return in the night proved that Daphne was somehow fixed in his mind. Would he be discouraged after two failures, scared away to seek some other quarry? Or would his obsession become more and more fixed upon Daphne herself? Daphne with her smooth brown skin, her lovely long throat that seemed sometimes bent forward by the weight of her hair, Daphne who must seem to his sick brain the symbol of all that was healthy and bright—the young Persephone whose innocence and youth, as she wandered through the Sicilian fields, had lured the King of Hell to drag her down with him into his own darkness and to put within her hands the gifts of forgetfulness and sleep.

The plaintive call of an owl came tremulously from the willows alongshore. Harold started. What would people think if he were found standing here by this tree staring up at the windows? He walked with careful naturalness around the side of the building and resumed his way along the street. But he knew what he must do. The idea had come to him just now as he stood there, though he hardly recalled the moment of its coming. Daphne herself must attract the murderer; she must be the bait that would lure him out of his dark hiding so that he might be caught and placed forever behind bars!

He was walking more quickly now, in a mood of tense excitement. Of course he would have to work out his plan: he would have to wait until tomorrow when the alcohol had left his system, but just now the scheme seemed so self-evident that he was amazed it had not occurred to him before.

His pace quickened still more. There were lights in few houses and almost no one on the streets. He must have been standing behind the apartment for a much longer time than he had imagined. Across the lake he could see the faint red lamps on a radio mast. He could hear a distant train, and as he paused to listen it seemed to carry his mind along with its soothing rush down gradual mysterious slopes into regions that he could hardly see.

If this suggestion made Daphne suffer, she had made him suffer through Dave Fulton. Of course he could not bear that she should suffer, even for a moment: it would be a kind of self-torture. But all that he would think of tomorrow. He would do nothing at any rate until he had talked with Edwin. The whistle of the train, faraway and long-drawn-out, flowed coolly through his head, relaxing, dissolving the knot of his thoughts and promising him sleep at last.

Next morning he had breakfast with Daphne on the Union Terrace. In the sunlight, among the gaily dressed students, the uniforms, his plan of the night before seemed remote and incongruous; especially so as he caught Daphne's smile and with it the sense once more of herself, as she actually was, a definite and very living person, undistorted by his own restless fantasy.

Well, he was committed to nothing. He had slept better last night than he had for some time, and he really enjoyed telling her about his interview with Paul.

"Of course I'm just about as far from the truth as I was before," he admitted, "except that I'm inclined to be a shade less suspicious of Paul. At least most of the time I am. He suggested that the napkin might have been dropped there on some other night entirely, which is certainly more plausible than the police suggestion that it was Terry or I who dropped it."

"Oh Harold!" she exclaimed. "I do hope that's so. It would be such a relief."

"It would mean we were much further from catching our man."

"But I'd rather we were. I'd rather he was never caught than to have it someone we know. To have it Paul or Edwin!"

He was on the point of asking her if she would rather have the man continuing to track her down, but her face had lightened so as he told her Paul's suggestion that he felt it would be too cruel.

83

"You never told me what you were doing Sunday," he remarked instead. "I was so busy talking that evening I didn't give you a chance."

He thought she hesitated a moment. "I was picnicking with Dave," she said. "I didn't mention it because I was so upset by what you were telling me about the murderer. For an instant even I had the awful feeling that it might be he, though of course I knew it couldn't be."

"It could be," Harold said, and he felt an unpleasant excitement around his heart. "Don't forget that. As you know, I don't think it is, any more than you do. But promise me that you won't take any chances."

"The last thing I want to do just now is to take chances," she said, and he felt that there was a shudder beneath her forced smile.

That afternoon Harold waylaid Edwin as he was leaving Main Hall. He had found out from University Information that Edwin had a class in Room 253 that let out at four-thirty, and he had waited for him by the bulletin board at the end of the corridor. One thing at least he had decided: he would not blurt out what he knew to Edwin as he had done to Paul. If it seemed best to tell him he would only do it later, after the most careful consideration.

It seemed to him that Edwin started slightly as he put his hand on his shoulder, but Edwin was the kind of person who might do that no matter how innocent.

"Hullo, Edwin!" he exclaimed. "I haven't seen you except in the distance since that fateful dinner party."

"What do you mean?" Edwin asked, and hurried on as if he had some special engagement.

"Our dinner at Terry's of course."

"And why was that particularly fateful?" His voice had the hint of snappishness that Harold was sure he must use with careless students.

"Oh, I was thinking of the attempted murder Daphne and I almost ran into afterwards. I sort of associate it with the dinner. Don't you?"

"I'm sure Jeanne and Terry would feel flattered," Edwin said. "No, I can't say that I do."

"Of course you weren't as near as we were. The scream

sounded almost on top of us, and I suppose it couldn't have been more than a hundred yards away. I don't think I've ever heard such a terrified scream. It keeps echoing in my mind. I hope to God they catch the man before he tries again, don't you?"

"Naturally," Edwin almost snarled. "What do you think I am? But I haven't the slightest idea he will try again. I still don't see what right you have to assume that this attempt was made by the original murderer."

"You mean that such things are catching?" Harold asked. "You could hardly say the second wasn't at least suggested by the first. Of course there's something in that. It's a perfectly valid point of view. A very interesting one."

They had been walking along the path between Main Hall and the lake, and now they were passing a little garden planted around a large juniper tree. Harold grasped Edwin's arm.

"Let's sit down on the bench over there for a few minutes," he said. "I've been thinking a good deal about these crimes. I'd be interested to hear your theories."

"I have no theories," Edwin said testily. "And as a matter of fact, the whole thing bores me to extinction."

"But you do have a theory," Harold contradicted. "You've just said you were convinced the attempt that night was not made by the first murderer. I'd really like to talk it over with you for a few minutes, unless of course you have some special personal reason for not wanting to talk about it."

He had pulled Edwin gently off the path and was leading him toward the garden bench.

"Of course I have no personal reason," Edwin protested. "What do you mean? It just doesn't interest me."

"I can realize that," Harold said, "although I must admit it interests me intensely, and I'm rather surprised that it bores you so, when you were almost involved in it yourself. It might just as well have been you that heard the scream. If you had been a little earlier it would have been. There were so many people wandering in the woods that night. But even if it doesn't interest you in itself, it must naturally interest you as an affair of public safety."

They had reached the bench, and Harold now sat down, pulling Edwin down next to him. On either side of them borders of zinnias, marigolds, and phlox glared in a blurred sheet of orange, pink, and magenta. The shadow of the juniper fell to the right of the bench, so that Harold and Edwin were in full sunlight. Harold could smell the aromatic bitterness of the juniper berries. A spike of feathery aster not yet in bloom brushed Harold's knee, and he noticed that each wiry stem was covered with a horde of bright red aphids, as if the plant were oozing blood. Surely they ought to be green!

"Of course as a citizen," Edwin said, "since you put it that way, I hope the murderer will be caught. But I don't see that it helps very much for amateurs to stick their noses into it. In fact, to be quite frank, it strikes me as just plain morbid."

"You artists," Harold exclaimed, "you live in such a special world that it's sometimes difficult for the layman to understand you. I suppose that as long as you can keep your own dream intact the rest of the universe can go hang."

"If you're bringing up the so-called 'artistic temperament,'" Edwin said, "I might as well tell you that I don't believe there is any such thing. I happen to play the piano. I suppose that's why you flatter me with the title of artist, because I can hardly believe it's because I teach English. Well, I play the piano because I like the sounds, and liking the sounds I've been interested enough to dip into the theory and try to understand something of the patterns which the sounds follow. I've got a certain technique, a very limited one, by practicing with a reasonable degree of care and patience, in very much the way you might practice your stance at golf, or your end game in chess. I remember saying the other night, since you brought up the subject, that you scientists have the most amazingly romantic ideas. I keep being impressed by it."

"I only meant," Harold said, "that you personally, for instance, strike me as living your real life in a world that is quite your own. Here we have a sensational murder, and two or three weeks later an attempt at a second one. You almost stumbled over that attempt, and yet it doesn't even

86

faintly interest you. It seems quite natural, no doubt. If a man's dream needs murder for its realization, well, that's his own affair. I can understand that—easily. I could even imagine your thinking that the victim should consider herself flattered. After all, she has been the inspiration of a wonderful moment. There must have been between the killer and herself the same instant of speechless and passionate intimacy that there is between the bullfighter and the bull, the same sense of being out of the world, absorbed into a private realm created from your own mind, or rather from both your minds, because it must be a work of collaboration. I suspect, Edwin, it's not the crime itself you find dull, but rather the clumsy way we laymen treat it as a mere crime, something involved with the law of the land, something that leads to the gallows or the asylum for the criminally insane, instead of an intimate, irreplaceable, aesthetic moment."

"Please!" Edwin exclaimed. "I suppose you realize that you're simply dishing out Montherlant diluted by Hemingway. My dear Harold, it's much too hot to be literary."

"I'm only trying to put myself inside your mind," Harold said. "Perhaps you could call that literary. It must be what the novelist attempts to do. But also the psychologist, and especially the psychiatrist. More and more I'm beginning to realize how inadequate they are. No matter how ingenious their theories, the reality they are trying to understand keeps slipping between them; perhaps because they don't realize that all their theories about human behavior, that all the feelings that color their so-called objective observations, are merely an intricate and devious system of self-justification. It may require some skill in cryptology to read them, but they can always be deciphered."

Harold paused as he noticed Edwin's face. He was staring downward across Harold's knees into the tall flowers that crowded around the bench. He seemed unaware of Harold's presence. His eyes were fixed and luminous as they sometimes were when he played the piano; his mustache quivered; his hands were clenched upon his knees so that the points of his knuckles made rosy spots against the bloodless skin.

87

Harold turned his head to follow that strange fixed glance. Barely a yard from his right knee, between a clump of magenta phlox and a tall orange zinnia, a ladder spider had woven its elastic web. A soft gray moth, almost an inch long, was struggling in the meshes, shaking the dust from its wings on to the threads in which it was entangled; and the spider, orange and black, with slender burnished legs, was slowly moving nearer, with a jerky sideways motion that shook the web like a cradle. The moth fluttered more vigorously. For a moment Harold could hear the desperate beat of its wings. A black pointed leg of the spider touched its body gently, with the sensitiveness of an expert dancer's, and then, with a twitch of the whole web, the spider leaped, the whirring of the wings ceased abruptly, and Harold could only imagine what sounds would come next if one had the ear to hear them.

He glanced at Edwin. His face looked haggard, and drops of sweat were pouring down his cheeks. He blinked, shook his head, and stared at Harold for an instant as if he did not recognize him.

"It's this heat," he said in a strange half whisper. "It's crazy to sit in the sun on a day like this."

Harold's own heart was pounding so violently that he was afraid Edwin might notice it. He felt sure that he was looking into the eyes of the murderer.

CHAPTER XI

AS SOON as Harold stepped into her hallway that same evening, Daphne could see that he had discovered something. After he had kissed her rather hurriedly he lit a cigarette, and she noticed that his hands were trembling. His eyes were unnaturally bright.

"What is it?" she asked, half dreading to hear his answer. "Did you see Edwin?"

"I saw him this afternoon," he said. "Yes."

"And you think it helped you?"

Harold had begun to pace the room. He stopped now and gave her a long look.

"I think he's our man," he said. "I'm almost sure of it."

Daphne felt no particular surprise or shock, simply because she was unable to realize emotionally what Harold had told her. He might have been making some historical statement, referring to the death of some king, the loss of some battle, which remained in her mind nothing but words, because the reality was so remote. It was impossible to associate Edwin as she knew him with the gray airless forest through which she roamed in her dreams.

"But Harold, how can you know?" she asked after an instant. "You might guess perhaps, but how can you be so sure?"

"I didn't say I was sure," he corrected her. "I only said I was almost sure."

"But what did he say? What did he do, to give you this idea?"

"I know at any rate that he gets the greatest excitement from watching the spectacle of terror and the destruction of life. In other words, he has a marked sadistic impulse."

"If he said anything to give you that impression, I'm sure he was just talking for effect. I could imagine Edwin's doing that—being very dry and ironical, if he guessed why you were questioning him."

"It was nothing he said," Harold explained. "I simply had the luck to be there when he noticed one of those big ladder spiders approaching a moth in its web. It was not a pretty sight—neither the spider nor Edwin."

For a moment from somewhere behind her picture of the familiar harmless Edwin there appeared another, a new one, so quickly gone that she could hardly tell what he looked like. He had merely signaled to her in recognition, as if to remind her that everything familiar and comforting was only a deluding film over the depths where they would meet again, the depths through which all life at every moment was blindly, helplessly groping. Then Edwin was himself once more, and the room, dappled with warm pink sunlight, was the room she had always known.

"I can imagine that it wasn't pretty," Daphne said, "but I don't see that that is very much to go on. Isn't such an impulse a fairly common one, especially in children? I ad-

89

mit Edwin seems a trifle queer. I could easily believe that in some ways he may be still living in his childhood."

"Of course such an impulse is common," Harold exclaimed. "To a certain extent, I suppose you could call it universal. But not to the extent that Edwin showed it—not even in a normal boy."

"All right," Daphne said. "Let's admit he is definitely abnormal. Even that doesn't surprise me very much. But does it follow that because he gets a thrill watching a spider kill a moth, he's also a murderer?"

Harold paused again in front of her. "Of course it doesn't!" he said, and she felt that her objections irritated him. "But it's a question of probabilities. Certainly it would be something of a coincidence if among the five men at the dinner party there were two who were abnormally sadistic, even if they revealed their sadism in different ways. And remember that for us there seems to be all the difference in the world between the merely childish cruelty of enjoying the death struggles of a moth, and the delight of shedding human blood—the compelling urge to murder. But that is partly because of our human laws; because there is no penalty for the first, and the penalty for the second is death or life imprisonment."

"But even from Edwin's point of view there must be a difference," she said.

"From the point of view of the sadist, the difference is not nearly so great. The death of the moth to him isn't just the unpleasant trifle it would seem to you; and on the other hand the murder of the young girl isn't an abominable crime, at least at the moment of its accomplishment. It's the yielding to an urge which for him is quite natural, which he cannot avoid. It's the escape at no matter what risk from an unbearable tension, like the tension of a drug addict deprived of his drug. It's the only thing that can bring him peace. Of course, like anyone else, the sadist may be a specialist: he may be interested only in torturing animals, or flunking students, or sending anonymous letters. But let's take the case of Edwin. Suppose that after months, perhaps years, of a perfectly hellish struggle, he makes his first kill. He is able to sleep peacefully; his mind is swept

90

clean at last, and life once more becomes worth living. After a period of several weeks he tries a second time, and fails. He tries to enter your room, and again fails. He must be desperate. It would seem to me that in such a state he could easily see in the agony of the moth, the triumphant approach of the spider, a symbol of his own desires. He could find it enormously exciting, because for him it is merely the representation of something else—a kind of prologue, like the dumb show in the play Hamlet contrives for his stepfather, that enacts the murder in pantomime before the players begin to speak their lines."

Daphne had hardly listened to the last part of what Harold had been saying, both because she knew the more she took it in the more uncomfortable she would feel, and because she had become so fascinated in watching his face. His eyes had been fixed upon her intently and yet he hardly seemed to see her. His features seemed lighted from within; they might almost, at the last, have been reflecting Edwin's face as he watched the spider; and she felt more than ever, as she realized his truly passionate interest in the case, how unreasonable she had been in making him promise to ignore it.

"But suppose it were Edwin," she said, "suppose you were absolutely sure of it—I don't see how you can prove it. I don't see how you can connect him with either crime."

Harold flung his cigarette into the fireplace.

"I've been thinking of that," he said. "We'll talk of it later, but now let's have a drink. And then I thought we might drive out to the Chicken Shack for dinner. How does that strike you?"

"I'd love it!" Daphne exclaimed. "At least all of it except talking any more about Edwin. Of course you must go ahead, Harold. You must do whatever you think you should; but won't it be enough if I don't scold you, and wish you the best of luck? Can't we make a bargain that you won't mention it here? It's not as if I could help you, you know."

Harold had turned from the fireplace and gone into the kitchen. "I promise I won't mention it to you except in so far as you can help me," he said.

It was a relief to be driving out through the country in Harold's open car. They had spent some time over their cocktails; Daphne had taken several, to cheer her up, and now the sun was near the horizon on the far side of the lake; the yellow grainfields, the patches of woodland were stained plum color, and rosy streamers trailed across the deep blue zenith. Daphne loved the way the wheat was piled in groups of little bundles leaning against each other. They suggested already, in spite of the heat, that autumn was not far away, and that soon the corn too would be gathered into shocks, the leaves of the oaks and maples would be flushing to bronze and scarlet, unless they were so dry that this year they would turn only to brown. She could understand as never before how a corroding and incessant worry might drive one to drink.

Her mood of vague gaiety lasted through dinner; she enjoyed the fried chicken, the mashed potatoes and salad. Their table was in a little screened-in summer-house that overlooked the road and the woods beyond. There was only one other table out there and by the time their apple pie was served, the group of students who had been eating there had left. It was nearly dark. The headlights of passing cars were turned on, and moths knocked softly against the wire screens.

"Daphne," Harold said abruptly, and before he went any further she knew that he was going to speak of the murder, "I promised you I wouldn't mention this business to you unless you could help me. But what if you could help me?"

She felt as if the glow from the cocktails, the lazy pleasantness of the dinner, had been switched off like an electric light.

"How could I possibly help you?" she asked, and tried not to scowl.

"You could help me a great deal," he said. "In fact I think that through you, and only through you, we can get our man."

Daphne tried now deliberately to find refuge in the disbelief she had felt when Harold in the apartment before dinner had been speaking of Edwin; but here in this dimly lighted summerhouse, with the moths beating against the

92

screens, the great dark woods just across the road, she felt that anything might be possible—that Edwin, that Paul Hatfield, that even Dave, might not be themselves, that anything might change horridly without warning into something else. And this suggestion of Harold's that she could help catch the murderer—it was like the first mysterious hint of a doctor that some major operation might be necessary: you could not bear to ask him what it was or when it must be; but you remembered as belonging to some carefree other world the banal illustrations in the magazine you were glancing at in the waiting room not five minutes ago.

"How could it be through me?" she asked, and her voice sounded in her ears as if someone else were speaking.

He leaned forward with his elbows on the table, his eyes staring into her face.

"It was you that gave me the first idea of it," he said, "when you told me you felt that he had marked you down. The fact that he has tried twice to get you makes me feel that you were perfectly right, and I was wrong when I didn't take your suggestion seriously. Daphne, I want to use you as a decoy."

"A decoy!" she repeated; and as she looked into his intent face staring at her, so near, so familiar, she shrank back suddenly as if Harold were himself the enemy. "You mean you want to use me as bait, Harold, like the kid that's tied to a stake to attract the leopard?"

He smiled, but it was a quick mechanical smile. "I hope you will attract the leopard," he said, "but otherwise the comparison doesn't hold. Because the kid is generally sacrificed, or so I should imagine, and you would be luring the murderer to his own destruction in order to save yourself, to set yourself free."

She felt that it would still take several minutes before she realized quite what Harold was suggesting, before her mind caught up with her emotions.

"But what would you want me to do?" she asked. "The whole idea sounds fantastic."

"On the contrary," he said, "it seems to me very practical. I'd want you to be walking somewhere, probably through the wood around Terry's, because that is where he

93

has struck both times, and he must associate it with his killing. I would see in some way that Edwin knew you were to be there. I would be there myself, probably with others, but that Edwin would not know. At the first sign of anything suspicious in his behavior the hunters would appear and the leopard would be caught before he had the chance to spring."

"But suppose it is not Edwin," she said faintly. "Even you admitted you were not sure."

"If it's not Edwin, there will be at any rate nothing lost, and we can start over again with some other plan."

"Nothing lost!" she exclaimed, and suddenly she felt that her face was flushing, her lips were swelling with anger. "Do you realize what such a thing would mean for me? Do you realize that each moment would be so frightening that I can hardly bear to think of it? I can't imagine how you can suggest such a scheme, Harold. And supposing it is Edwin, how can you be sure you wouldn't be too late? It doesn't take very long to draw a knife, you know."

"It seems to me that the risk would be slight," he said, "especially when you compare it with the risk you are now actually running all the time. And as for your fear, don't you imagine I can realize what this would mean for you? I'd be feeling myself every instant of your terror. Your suspense would be no worse than mine, because we would be sharing it, Daphne—the suspense, and the agony and the triumph."

He reached across the table and seized her wrist. "That would be something," he said, "wouldn't it, Daphne? Will you do it?"

She pulled her arm away from him.

"No," she exclaimed with concentrated fierceness. "I certainly will not! And I don't see how you could ever ask me to do it."

She got up from the table, but Harold remained seated, following her only with his eyes.

"You realize, Daphne," he said in a very quiet voice which made her sound all the noisier in her own ears, "that it would not be only yourself that you were saving. It might be any number of other girls, whom he will be stalking

94

through those woods. Or perhaps he will climb through their bedroom windows when they are asleep. It would be quite a shock to you, wouldn't it, if you should read in the paper one of these afternoons that another girl had been found slashed to death?"

Daphne sank down into her chair again, and as she tried to speak she burst into tears.

"I don't see how you can talk this way," she sobbed. "I don't see how you can torment me like this. It almost seems as if you did it on purpose. But if you think he would be after others, if you think I could save them and put an end to this horror, perhaps I can make myself do it, Harold. I don't know. I can't tell you now. Let's go home, and then perhaps tomorrow I can tell you."

They drove home in almost complete silence. "He shouldn't have asked me," Daphne kept thinking. "He never should have asked me to do it." And when he kissed her good night she was quite unresponsive to his lips.

She lay awake for a long time on the cot in Gerty's living room, listening to the shrill ironic chirping that seemed now to have been always ringing in her ears. "If only Mother were living," she thought, "how different everything would be! If I could only talk this over with someone!" She thought of Terry, but she would hesitate to speak to him, because she felt that he was rather Harold's friend than hers. Then she thought of Dave. Dave surely must like her; in fact she knew he did, so why pretend to doubt it? There would be something very comforting in discussing it with Dave; he was at once so breezy and so sensible. It occurred to her that from what Harold had said, Dave, or Terry for that matter, might himself be the man they were seeking— but no, she would not take that into consideration: if she had to suspect everyone, everyone she was fond of, she would drive herself crazy.

When she fell asleep at last, she dreamed again of the dry gray woods, but this time the avenues of trees were more like metal corridors, the long dim passageways on a ship, perhaps, though no ship could contain such interminable windings. Perhaps it was really a prison. If she met someone she would inquire. But she would not have to in-

95

quire, because she had known from the first that it was a madhouse.

The next morning she called up Dave. It was not until she heard his answering voice that she realized quite how much she had depended on his being there. "Hullo," he said, and the word sounded like a gruff sleepy yawn.

"Dave," she said, "I didn't rout you out of bed?"

"Daphne, how wonderful!" She almost smiled at the sudden change in his tone.

"I was wondering if you could meet me at the hospital today?" she asked. "I know you're apt to be there, but there was something special I wanted to ask you about."

"I'll *be* there," he exclaimed. "Thanks for calling. My day's a success already."

When she stepped out of the hospital elevator, Dave was there waiting for her.

"This is swell!" he said. "You don't know what a lift you gave me this morning. Where shall we go? You look warm. Would you like a coke or a glass of beer to cool you off?"

"No, thanks," she said. "At least not now. I thought we might walk along the lake shore for a little."

"Fine! There's nothing I'd like better."

For the first time in nearly two weeks, except for the single thunderstorm, the sky was overcast; a warm sluggish wind rustled the reeds and passed in silvery ripples through the willow branches. Daphne hardly knew how to begin. She wished Dave would ask her why she had called him, but she was sure that he would be too tactful. They had come upon a flock of mallards among the lily pads in the bay and Dave had been telling her about a pet drake he had owned when he was ten years old.

"Dave," she said suddenly, "you must have wondered what I wanted to ask you about."

"To tell you the truth," he said, "I was so pleased you wanted to ask me about anything, I haven't wasted much time wondering what it was."

"It's not really very much, I guess, but I *have* been disturbed, Dave. I'm afraid you may think I'm an awful coward."

96

"Nonsense!" he exclaimed. "But what is it, **Daphne?** Don't hesitate if you want to tell me, if you think I can help you in any way at all. I wish you knew how flattered it makes me feel."

Then as she looked into his kind dark eyes, she wondered why she had hesitated, and without mentioning Edwin's name or explaining why a particular man was under suspicion, she told him of Harold's plan for using her as a decoy.

"You *will* think I'm a coward," she said again, "because I simply can't bear the idea, and yet I suppose I must do it. Don't you think I must, Dave?"

"I think the whole idea is outrageous," he exclaimed. "You musn't consider it, Daphne. God, but I'm glad you told me about it!"

His words filled her with a glow of comfort; and yet the next instant she realized that she would probably do as Harold wanted. Perhaps it was the fact that Dave, that most people, might consider there was no need for her to do it that made it seem possible. If it had been something that she had had to do, that anyone in the circumstances would have done, then she might not have dared; but you could screw your courage to the sticking point to perform something exceptional. She had always felt it would be easier for her to rescue a child from a burning building than to have old Dr. Hathaway pull an impacted tooth.

"But Dave," she said, "I feel that I ought to do anything I possibly can. If this man is a mass murderer, as Harold is convinced he is, he may keep on attacking any number of other girls. And if he is not, then there is nothing for me to worry about."

"It's not the idea of using a decoy," Dave said. "That may be good or it may not. I wouldn't know. It's the idea of using *you*. There must be women detectives. Or, I've read of policemen dressing up as women to trap men of this sort. Let Harold get one of them, and it's all right with me."

"I'm sure Harold must have considered that, but he doesn't think it would work. His theory is, you see, that I'm the one the murderer is really after."

"If you ask me," Dave said violently, "Harold's crazy.

No sane man would ask you to do a thing like that, especially if he was in love with you."

"Aren't you being rather unjust to Harold?" Daphne asked, annoyed at this attack, all the more so because it made her feel that perhaps her speaking to Dave had been disloyal. "Don't forget that if he's so eager to catch this man, and I should think you would be too, it's mostly on my account."

"I don't believe it," Dave said. "It's partly a kind of morbid fascination and partly pure vanity."

"Dave!" she protested. "I won't let you talk like that. What's got into you?"

It was as if he were forcing her against her will to conspire with him against Harold.

"What's got into me! It's just when I think of anyone's putting you in such a position! Of anyone's deliberately exposing you to this . . . this moronic murderer, I can't be polite, that's all. But you musn't do it, Daphne. In fact, I won't let you do it!"

"You won't let me!" she exclaimed, and it was as if all her anger of last night had been suddenly transferred from Harold to Dave. "I'd like to see you stop me. What right have you to tell me what I can do? I asked for your opinion. I wasn't asking for orders. And then you begin to talk in this mean way about Harold! It only makes me feel that I shouldn't have spoken to you in the first place. I certainly shall do whatever Harold suggests. I trust him completely."

"That's more than I do," Dave said angrily, "but it's your own funeral."

"Yes, it is," she said, and again she knew that she was losing control. "It's certainly no concern of yours. Goodby."

She turned quickly but Dave seized her arms.

"Daphne, I won't let you go like this," he said. "I didn't mean that last. It was just because I was so upset about you. Can't you understand?"

Daphne struggled to break away.

"It's you that don't understand," she said, half sobbing, "or you'd let me go at once. You don't understand me! You don't understand Harold! You don't understand how I feel

98

about him! Don't you see you're making me hate you?"

Her voice had risen hysterically, and now she shook herself free.

He did not follow her. As she walked swiftly back along the shore, she noticed the dust of the path becoming pitted with dark brown spots, and could feel a few warm drops on her face, that mingled with her tears.

As soon as she reached home she called Harold.

"Harold," she said, "I'll do whatever you want, but don't tell me what it is until it's all arranged. And try to have it soon—as soon as possible. I think I'd rather not see you until it *is* arranged. It's not because I'm angry, but I'd only keep wondering what you were thinking and planning, and I don't think I could bear it."

After she had hung up, she remained for a moment sitting by the telephone. Outside her window the glossy hickory leaves were softly battered by the rain. The rooms were already growing dusky. It would soon be night.

CHAPTER XII

*I*T MUST have been after eleven o'clock. Gerty and Mary were both in bed, and Daphne lay half asleep on the cot in their living room when she heard a quiet knocking. It was repeated a moment later, soft but businesslike, and she decided that she would call one of the girls; but then she realized that the knock was not on the door of this room, which opened on to the landing, but on the door of her own apartment directly across the hall.

She wondered if it were Harold, come in spite of her telling him not to, to bid her good night. She hoped it was; she would be glad to see him now.

She got out of bed and was putting on her kimono when she remembered that Harold knew she was not sleeping in her own room. He might be taking the chance, of course, that she was still there; but she waited until the knock was repeated a third time, and now that she was wide awake it struck her that this did not sound like Harold's knock: it was too subdued, too precise, as if it had been struck by some neat and economical machine. Could it be Dave, coming to apologize? Would he dare to come so late? She told herself that this would be outrageous of him, but she could not still feel angry. Even Dave she would love to see for a few minutes, if it were only to scold him.

She stepped to the door and called cautiously: "Harold?"

There was no answer.

"Dave?" This time she tried to make her tone sound more severe.

There was silence except for the steady rain on the leaves. She waited a minute, two minutes, standing there just inside Gerty's door. Was this night caller still waiting outside, a few feet away? If his errand were important, and it almost must be for him to come so late, why didn't he answer her? Why should her being here with Gerty and Mary make any difference?

A train whistle, eerie and far away, floated to her through the rustling leaves, from out of the depths of the night; and suddenly she began to tremble so violently that she was afraid whoever stood outside, if he were still there, might hear her. Of course it made all the difference that she was with Mary and Gerty. The errand that had brought her visitor in from the outer darkness was one of those that must be accomplished without witnesses.

Still shaking through her whole body, she crept back into bed and it seemed to her that for hours and hours she listened to the rain on the leaves.

When she opened her eyes in the morning the sun was shining into her room. Her panic of the night before seemed to her now rather hysterical; after all, the explanation might be quite harmless. Perhaps the stranger on the landing had guessed he had disturbed her and stolen away, just as you may guiltily hang up the telephone at eight o'clock in the morning when you feel that the person answering you has been roused from bed. This was what she must try to make herself believe.

On her way to the Red Cross she noticed how much cleaner and fresher everything looked: it was as if a dusty window had been raised and she were seeing the trees, the

100

grass and the clouds, the sidewalks, the fronts of the houses, for the first time in days without anything between herself and them. But the heat was still there—a damper heat now, that made her think of the South Seas, of Guadalcanal and Salamaua. And this made her once more ashamed of what a coward she was proving herself to be.

She worked hard all morning at her bandages, ate lunch alone downtown, and was walking back toward the hospital when someone hailed her from a car. It was a smart-looking woman in black whom she recognized only after a moment as Wanda Hatfield.

"Get in," Wanda said. "I'll give you a lift."

"You know I'm afraid I put my foot in it," Wanda said, when they had driven a few blocks. "I happened to mention to Harold the other evening that you had been off all day with Dave. I never dreamed that you were keeping it secret."

"I wasn't," Daphne said shortly. "I told Harold about it. Why shouldn't I? Or why should I, for that matter?"

"Why indeed?" Wanda said. "If you told him, it must have been after he dined with us, because it seemed to come as something of a surprise. You know how men are—so possessive! I mentioned it just now because I like Harold and I'd hate to have him quarrel with Dave. Dave and I are *very* good friends, as you probably have guessed."

"I can't say that I had." Daphne's tone was sharp. "Certainly not from Dave's own actions. I imagine he'd behave in very much the same way to any woman much older than he."

Wanda chuckled.

"My dear girl," she said, "you seem to be rather on edge this morning. I had no idea I was probing a tender spot."

"Not at all," Daphne said angrily.

She knew that she was flushing, and felt thankful that the hospital was not far away. It did seem too much that she should have run into Wanda on top of everything else. Next thing she would be in tears again! She had broken down two or three times recently with Harold, and yesterday with Dave, and she simply despised it.

"Dave loves to tell me of his little affairs," Wanda went

101

on after a minute. "I scold him but he's incorrigible. Fortunately I'm not of a jealous temperament."

She drew up to the curb in front of the hospital.

"I'd have Terry or someone look over you, dear," she said as Daphne reached for the door of the car. "If I were Harold I'd feel quite worried about you. You look terribly tired. You don't by any chance feel qualmish when you wake up in the mornings?"

Daphne got out of the car without speaking. On the sidewalk she turned and stared fiercely up at Wanda.

"Thank you very much for your *kindness,*" she said, and felt that the ironic stress she put on the word, to make up for the stinging retort she could not think of, was childishly ineffective.

She was glad that she was assigned to the men's surgical ward that afternoon, because it was the one in which she had to work the hardest, and because she was apt to run into Terry Macfarlane. He came up to her during her last half hour, as she was changing the very dirty sheets of a poor old man full of tubes. The hearty kindness of his voice was more comforting to her than it had ever been.

"When you've finished your job," he said, "lay off for awhile and we'll smoke a cigarette on the balcony. I haven't seen you this last week."

A few minutes later she found him waiting for her, leaning against the railing.

"You know, Daphne," he said, "I think you're losing weight. We'll have to put you on a diet if you don't begin to plump up a bit. I think you're working too hard."

"It's not that," she said. And then she smiled. "Mrs. Hatfield said something like it a few hours ago. She gave me a lift."

"Wanda?" Terry chuckled. "I can imagine the way it was slanted. Didn't you notice how she was glowering at you at our house, because Dave Fulton fell for you?"

"No, I didn't," Daphne said; and then trying to speak as casually as she could, she went on: "Is there anything special between Dave and her? I mean . . . does she consider him her own private property?"

Terry laughed. "There may be between her and Dave,"

he said, "but certainly not between Dave and her. She's been chasing the poor fellow for the last six months, but I don't worry much about him. He's quite able to look out for himself."

For a moment Daphne felt almost gay. She was delighted that Wanda Hatfield had not been able to get Dave into her clutches; and she realized that her fear of such a thing —though she never actually had believed it—had made her forgive Dave for yesterday. In fact when she thought of their talk by the lake what she regretted most was the way her voice had risen almost to a scream. She would love to walk by the Hatfield's house in intimate conversation with Dave, while Wanda stared at them through the front window.

"I tell you what," Terry said a few minutes later, as Daphne tossed her cigarette over the balcony into the bed of zinnias far below, "why don't you and Harold come out and dine with us again on Saturday? That's day after tomorrow. Jeanne has spoken of you a lot. You made quite a hit with her, young woman, and Jeanne is apt to be pretty damn choosy, in spite of the fact that she married me. Or perhaps that was what taught her her lesson."

"I'd love to," Daphne said. "I don't know about Harold. You'll have to ask him."

"If you will come," Terry said, and patted her on the back, "I don't worry much about Harold. I'll call him when I get home, and you tell him if you see him in the meantime."

Dave was not waiting for her this afternoon, and she wondered whether it was because he was angry or because he was afraid that she would be. Harold did not come to take her to dinner, which was only natural since she had told him he shouldn't; but as she boiled herself an egg at about nine o'clock, she felt again the almost sickening loneliness she had felt the night before. She wrote another long letter to Barbara that evening, but it was hard to give it even a touch of gaiety.

The air was so damp and close that it was a relief. as she moved across to Gerty's and Mary's room, to hear thunder far away to the south. She hurried to get into bed before

103

the storm should arrive, because she always felt safest in bed. But the thunder came no nearer, though several times during the night she was half wakened by its distant rumblings.

The next morning while she was washing her breakfast dishes the telephone rang and she answered it eagerly. It was Harold, but his voice had the kind of excitement she had grown to dread.

"Terry says you told him you'd come to dinner there tomorrow night," he said quickly. "He asked me too, and of course I accepted. And darling, it gives us a wonderful chance to try our little trap."

"Already!" she exclaimed, her heartbeats quickening.

"You told me to arrange it as soon as I could, and I've been thinking about it most of the night. That's why I didn't call you yesterday. I wanted to be quite sure of it. Listen. Here it is. I told you I've accepted, and I'll go. But I'll make a point of running into Edwin; I'll bring up the subject and ask him if he's invited. I know he isn't. Terry said there'd be nobody but us. I'll give him some plausible reason why I can't make it myself, but I'll tell him you're going without me. I'll say that I hope you don't insist on walking home. It would be just like you, out of bravado, if nothing else; you're so darn independent."

"But it wouldn't be like me," she said urgently. "And no sane person would believe I'd do it. I may be quarrelsome, but I wouldn't dream of deliberately walking home through the woods where I might meet a murderer."

"You just said, 'No sane person would believe it,'" Harold went on with growing excitement. "But remember that if Edwin is our man, he's not wholly sane. His vanity, not to speak of his desire, which by now must be quite desperate, will persuade him easily enough that you might walk into his trap. And of course he has no idea that we suspect the murderer is concentrating on you. I might even suggest that it would be a friendly thing if he strolled out in that direction on the chance of meeting you. Or it might be better not. I'll have to think it over. You see, if I didn't go, Terry would insist on driving you in. As it is, we'll say good night, and start out together; then I'll leave you just

104

beyond the gate and take to the woods. There is where I must be careful: not to run into Edwin, but there shouldn't be much risk of that, because he will be coming from the other direction—that is if he comes at all. It may not work out, but I think it's worth the try. How does it strike you?"

"I can't tell," she said listlessly, "because I can't make it seem real. But Harold, I think he . . . I think the murderer came to see me last night . . . very late, when he would find me alone."

"He did?" Harold's tone was immensely excited. "How do you know? What makes you think so?"

She told him then about her midnight visitor.

"You see!" Harold exclaimed, and there was a ring of triumph in his voice, which might have angered her if she had had the energy to be angry—"You see! It's just as I thought! He can hardly wait. But dearest I'm crazy to see you—more than ever now. May I come to dinner tonight? We can take a vacation from murder. I promise not to mention it, or anything to do with it."

"Yes," she said. "Come to dinner, Harold. I've been very lonely."

"I'll try to see Edwin at lunch today," he said. "The worst thing that could happen would be for him to run into Terry and happen to mention that I'd said I couldn't be there tomorrow. But that's most unlikely, even if they should meet; and I don't suppose they see each other for weeks on end."

That afternoon Dave again did not turn up at the hospital. Daphne felt that she would have been very much disappointed, if Harold were not coming to dinner. "If only he keeps his promise," she thought, "and doesn't bring up the crimes! If only he will be the way he used to be!" She told herself that he must know what he was about: perhaps her own danger, as long as the murderer was uncaught, was even greater than she suspected; perhaps there would be a cordon of police hidden in the woods. She simply must not think of it. She must draw in deep breaths of indifference, of her present numb disbelief, as the patient eagerly inhales the anesthetic, although he feels that it is choking him to death.

She had not started directly home, because her rooms now seemed lonely and strange, and she would rather avoid them until just before Harold's arrival. She was walking along the edge of a little park not far from the hospital when she heard the sound of a piano from the open window of a small brick apartment building just ahead of her. At once she realized that this was where Edwin lived, and recognized for the first time that a dim and perverse curiosity, like the impulse which directs a sleepwalker, had been guiding her steps in this direction.

The music was very peaceful and stately; she thought she recognized some of the old French airs he had been playing the night of the dinner. It gave her an odd sensation—not so much of fear as of suspense, of a dreamlike unreality—to think that the man who was making that music might have tried once to kill her, might possibly try again. She started to hurry by, but the music fascinated her. How could those lovely, those unearthly sounds be connected with murder? She remembered once when she was a little girl running ahead of Mother through the woods and finding the most beautiful mushroom she had ever seen. It had a pure white stem with a neat frill around it, and a scarlet top that shaded into gold about the edge and was scattered with silvery flecks like sugar or snow. She had thought it must be a fairy's house and was bending over it in delight when Mother called to her sharply that she must not touch it, that it was deadly poison. After that, whenever she found such a mushroom, she would stand as near it as she dared and wonder just where the poison was, in the frill or the lovely red color or perhaps in those white flecks, and wonder if it would hurt her if she stroked it very gently, or what it would taste like if she nibbled the tiniest crumb. And just because she knew it was poisonous, it seemed to her more beautiful than ever, like a lovely princess in a fairy tale, who was not really a princess at all but an evil witch.

Daphne realized that she was standing still. Her eye noticed a wooden bench, across the street from the apartment, at the edge of the shaded turf. She walked slowly back to it, and almost in spite of herself sat down to listen.

The park, a circle of grass scattered with a few big oaks, was empty. Sunlight slanted over the turf between the trees, and among the blades at her feet she could see the crumbling remnants of last year's acorns. Squirrels ran across the grass from one tree to another. The music seemed to be flowing like the gentlest breeze among the old tree trunks, among the quiet, listening leaves. It made everything seem unreal and transitory; the park, the houses, might dissolve like a mirage, might pass out of space entirely, as this day, even while she sat here, was passing out of time—and what would be left? A vast and resigned sadness, a loneliness such as you could only imagine if no one else in the world existed, if you were set down, the only living thing, amid the emptiness of a lifeless planet.

The music stopped. Daphne felt tears flowing from her eyes. She would not, she could not make herself believe, no matter what Harold thought, that the man who could play like that was a murderer—that if she had opened her door last night it was he she would have found silently waiting.

"Why Daphne! I didn't know you were out there!"

She gave a start, and looked over her shoulder. Edwin was leaning from the window. She tried to smile at him, as if to atone for Harold's suspicions, but she felt that her face must look queer.

"I've been listening for quite awhile," she called. "It's beautiful."

"Wait a second," he said. "I'll join you. The room is too much of a mess to ask you in."

Should she run away? But no, that would be mad. Nothing could happen here in broad daylight, with people passing by. Should she simply get up from the bench and walk on? In that case she should have told Edwin not to come out.

The door opened. There he was. He was crossing the street. . . . But of course he was only Edwin—harmless, sensitive Edwin, who could play so beautifully that it sometimes made you cry. Any other idea did not belong to real life but to a dim nightmare world that was inside your own head. Nonetheless, she had to force herself not to draw away from him when he sat down beside her.

107

"What were those pieces?" she asked quickly, as if to seek refuge in the music. "Weren't they the same things you were playing the other night at Terry's?"

"Some of them were. They were all old French. Chambonnières. D'Anglebert, Roberday."

"They are very sad, don't you think so?"

"Most of them are dance tunes," he told her, "but I can understand how some of them might sound melancholy."

"Don't you think so yourself?"

"When I play," he explained, "it's very hard for me to tell exactly what emotions I feel—I mean ordinary human emotions. There is feeling, of course, intense feeling in all great music, but it's apt to be a purely musical thing. Of course it is related to your feelings of every day, toward yourself and toward other people, and I've no doubt that you may give away your mood to a sympathetic listener more than you sometimes imagine."

"If that's the case," Daphne said, "you must be very lonely."

He sent her a swift look, and she wondered if he resented her remark.

"I'm sometimes lonely," he said, and his voice had all at once taken on its habitual dryness, "but I imagine many people are. Loneliness is part of our human predicament; unless, that is, you're a mere brute member of the great crowd and have nothing that could be called an individual life. I imagine ants and tent caterpillars are never lonely."

She laughed. "I don't believe they are ever what you could call happy either," she said.

"No, I doubt if they have the capacity for really intense enjoyment."

Daphne rose from the bench. She was certainly not afraid, but she was excited; she was a little dizzy. "Well," she said. "I must be going on. Thanks again, Edwin."

"It's strange that you should have come here this afternoon," he remarked as he rose with her, "because I happened to be having lunch today with Harold. He tells me you're going to be at Terry's tomorrow night."

"Yes, I am."

"He told me that he can't be there himself."

"No," she said, and wondered what reason Harold had given.

"If you should be walking home," he said, "around half-past ten or thereabouts I might join you, if you don't mind. I'm very fond of those woods, and I love walking at night."

"You mustn't think of putting yourself out for me," she said quickly, and hoped her voice sounded natural.

"It wouldn't be putting myself out, I assure you. It would be the greatest pleasure."

As she glanced at his face—impassive, faintly smiling—she felt a sensation of cold creep outward through her body to her finger tips. For that moment the other Edwin stood again before her, beckoning her ironically, from across a nightmare chasm, to join him in that dry gray region where he prowled alone.

CHAPTER XIII

*A*S HAROLD and she entered the Macfarlanes' gateway, Daphne remembered sharply how she had walked between these white posts on that evening two weeks ago, and how thankful she had been to get here. She had thought then that her ordeal was over, and yet it had only begun. Perhaps tonight when she went to bed, after her lonely walk through the woods, it would really be over. Or perhaps she would never reach her bed.

Though the air was just as hot tonight, the lawn was greener than it had been the last time and there were no sprinklers playing. The white house with its tall pillars looked brilliantly clean, almost shining, in the evening light. It made her think of some huge wedding cake whose frosting was beginning to grow sticky in the damp heat. Terry opened the door as they were walking up the steps on to the porch.

"You seem to pick hot nights!" he exclaimed. "But I guess they are all about as bad. Jeanne's making you mint juleps instead of cocktails. That's her specialty. I always encourage it, because then I can lie back and take it easy."

He led them into the big living room, and Daphne caught

herself glancing right away at the piano. This evening someone had placed on it a big bowl from which there rose the
stalks of pink spotted lilies. That was the only difference
tonight: last time there had been marigolds in the room.
She went to the piano and put her face as close to the lilies
as she dared without brushing off the thick red-brown pol-
len from their stamens. Their indescribable sweet perfume
was almost her favorite of all; and as she closed her eyes
she could imagine herself back in the garden at the farm,
with Barbara and Jimmy and perhaps Tim, with his tail in
the air, padding along over the grass behind them. It seemed
almost that if she could concentrate on that delicious sweet-
ness she could escape from this room, from tonight, from
these dark surrounding woods; and for a moment she could
not bear to raise her eyelids.

When she did turn to face the others, Jeanne was coming
through the dining room door with a tray on which stood
some tall frosted glasses, and Daphne realized that if she
had to be here there was no one she would rather see. She
had forgotten how much she liked Jeanne's face.

"Well, Daphne," Jeanne exclaimed, "I'm delighted to
see you! I'm glad you weren't scared away from here for
good. I should think you might have been."

The julep was delicious. Daphne had often read of them
but this was the first she had ever tasted. She had just begun to sip hers when she noticed Harold give a rather
startled look toward the door, and the next instant she
heard the sound of a car on the drive.

"That must be Paul," Jeanne said. "I'll go and make
his."

"Paul!" Harold exclaimed. "Are Paul and Wanda going
to be here? I didn't know it was a party."

"Just Paul," Terry said. "He horned in on us, the old
rascal. I happened yesterday to mention you were coming
out here, and this afternoon he called up and said Wanda
had some bridge date, and couldn't he come along? He
bribed his way in with the promise of red coupons. I think
you were the attraction, Daphne. Last time it was Dave
who invited himself. You're a very sought-after young
lady."

"She is that," Harold said. "I'm beginning to feel I must keep my eye on her."

The next moment Paul stepped into the room, very neat in a straw-colored suit, with a yellow rosebud in his buttonhole.

"Good evening everyone," he said. He gave Harold a shrewd look and raised his eyebrows slightly. "My dear Harold," he exclaimed, "you seem rather taken aback. I hope you don't mind my being here."

"Why should I mind?" Harold asked. "If Jeanne and Terry can stand you, I guess I can make the effort."

"Harold and I had a most interesting talk the other day," Paul said. "Which reminds me, Harold, I happened to run into Edwin this noon. Or rather I looked him up. He's a queer fellow perhaps, but I find him interesting. I hadn't realized until quite recently how interesting. Harold and I had been talking about the murders," Paul went on to explain. "I don't know why I persist in thinking of them in the plural. Would you think I was frightfully rude, Terry, if I confessed that part of my reason for barging in on you tonight was—frankly—the morbid and naïve thrill of returning to the scene of the crimes?"

Terry laughed. "Good God, man!" he exclaimed. "To hear you talk, anyone would think I'd carved up the poor girl in the cellar."

Paul pursed his lips. "No-o," he said. "That hardly follows, though now that you mention it, I suppose she could have been carved up here, as you so vividly express it, and lugged into the thicket where she was found. I mean the first victim of course, the one he really got. No, I merely meant that the two attempts—the success and the failure—have cast a kind of special aura over this whole region. And then too"—he turned to Daphne—"I hoped I might have the pleasure of driving you home, my dear. I even thought, if we should hear any little owls, you might enjoy tracking one down with me. I remember you told me you were fond of them. Harold could wait in the car, if he didn't care to come along. I'm sure you would trust your fiancée with an aged man like me, eh Harold?" He cocked his small bright eye in Harold's direction.

"Daphne and I have a date to walk home." Harold said. "Don't we, darling?"

Just then Jeanne returned with Paul's drink.

"You're walking?" she exclaimed. "When you have the offer of a perfectly good car? Well, that's what it is to be young, although as I look back to my nonage it seems to me I was always as lazy as I am today. But I should think you'd be rather turned against walking home from here when you think of what you ran into the last time."

Terry laughed and patted Harold on the back. "If I know Harold," he said jovially, "he enjoyed every minute of it."

Daphne found the wine at dinner a great support. Though it could not really make her cheerful, it at least pushed the evening-to-come further off into a soft padded darkness, and limited her world to the circle of the candlelit table, a vague world in which people's faces became masks and voices blurred into rather pleasant sounds if you didn't have to grasp what they were saying. They were discussing what might happen in Italy now that Mussolini had fallen, and although she was able to answer direct questions, she felt that her replies were a kind of carry-over from a former stage of sobriety, like the cards with their name and address written on them that are given to small children to produce in case they are lost.

When dinner was through, however, and they went out on to the porch for coffee, the darkness of the lawn, the leafy smell of the invisible woods, brought her to herself with a shock. It was as if she had promised lightly that she would dive from a high place, and now found herself on the springboard fifty feet above the water, compelled to jump when the signal came, and knowing that she could not move, that she could not fling herself into that sickening void. The young moon must have set; the sky was clouded: the season for fireflies was over, and there was no light anywhere.

"Well, Harold," Terry remarked, after they had finished their coffee and been chatting for perhaps an hour, "if your theory is right, isn't it about time for our friend to strike again?"

112

"There haven't been enough attempts to see if he follows any special rhythm or cycle," Harold said, "but I shouldn't be surprised if we heard from him before long."

"I've sometimes wondered," Paul said in a meditative tone. "if in such a case one gets much pleasure beforehand from the mere contemplation of the crime, or if the fear of being caught and the necessity for cunning planning rather tend to spoil the picture. Of course that very fear might add to the excitement, just as no doubt the terror of the victim does when the moment arrives."

"In many cases," Harold said, "I believe that the main urge is toward the actual shedding of blood."

Daphne who was sitting next to Jeanne reached for her hand and grasped it convulsively.

"I see that I'll have to be dampening your spirits again," Jeanne said. "but from now on I absolutely taboo the subject of murder. If you want to talk of something that's both horrible and mysterious, I suggest the income tax."

It was not long after that that Paul got up from his chair.

"I won't be breaking up the party," he said, "because I never belonged to it, and I really must be getting home. This was sheer debauchery my coming tonight. I should have been in the laboratory. You're sure you won't ride, Daphne? Why not leave Harold if he's stubborn? It's good to put them in their place."

"No thanks," Daphne heard herself saying. "We really had planned to walk. But sometime I'd love to go after owls."

As she watched, a minute later, the lights from the car shining on the very green grass, sliding across the white gateposts, and then being swallowed up by the trees, she felt that her last chance of escape had vanished.

"And now, darling," Harold said in a few minutes, "I think we ought to be getting on ourselves. You seem rather tired, and we want to take it easy."

"I think she is tired," Jeanne said. "I've noticed it too. I tell you what, Daphne, why don't you spend the night here? We have lots of room, and it would be great sport having you here tomorrow."

It seemed to Daphne that she had never felt a greater

113

longing to do anything: it was as if an angel had suddenly appeared to her and offered to take her, without any fuss or strangeness, directly to heaven. For an instant the night seemed darker than ever, so dark that it became a tangible wall which she could not push her way through; but again her voice of itself came to her rescue.

"I'd love to," she said, "but I really can't this time, Jeanne. I hope, though, you'll ask me again."

"Of course I will. Soon. Good night."

"Good night."

She was walking down the drive with Harold, clinging so firmly to his arm that she felt she must be holding him back. Once they were out of the lee of the house she felt a sluggish wind, and as they passed between the gateposts into the road she began to hear a steady faint rustle that came from all sides, like the swish of water around a boat. Suddenly a whippoorwill called several times, as it had called the other night; a second answered it; and then from far away she heard the lonely quavering of an owl and wondered if it were Mr. Hatfield trying to call one to him.

They had walked a few paces down the little road when Harold stopped.

"Now, dearest," he said, "all you have to do is keep walking, at a natural pace. Remember I'll be very near you, and I've got my automatic. This breeze is a fine thing because it covers the rustling anyone might make in the undergrowth. There's a good chance nothing will happen."

He pulled her almost fiercely against him.

"Can you feel how my heart is pounding?" he asked in a low voice. "I'm sure yours is too."

Then before she could hold him back he stepped away from her so swiftly that she was not even sure at just what point he had entered the woods.

She walked on blindly as in a dream. "Harold is there," she kept repeating to herself. "He's there, he's very close. If I called, if I even spoke in my usual voice, he could hear me." After all, this ought not to be so frightening as that other walk along this road, because then she had been really alone. She could only see the road, vaguely lighter than the trees, for a few yards ahead of her. The rustling of the

114

leaves at moments became so marked that she was sure it must be Harold—Harold or someone else. Then it would subside as it had risen, and she could picture the night wind moving here and there in long dark ripples across the top of the woods.

The whippoorwill called again, far away to the right. Instinctively she turned her head in that direction, and when she glanced back at the road before her, she felt for a long instant her heart stop beating. From the corner of her eye she saw that someone was walking beside her.

She could not bear to turn her head toward him and yet she must. She tried to speak, but words for a moment would not come.

"Who is it?" she then asked, and was surprised to hear that she had whispered.

"Did I startle you?"

The voice was Edwin's. It was no whisper and yet it had a whisper's intimate quality. There was even in it, it seemed to her, a kind of breathless amusement, which reminded her of something, something long ago. . . . Ah yes, she remembered now' it was the voice of a horrid little boy in seventh grade who used to try to murmur obscene stories into her ear when he sat beside her in study hour.

"Yes," she said faintly. "Yes, you did. A little."

"Only a little?" he asked. "That's good!"

For a full minute he did not speak again. Was Harold near? Why didn't he come out? But it would be too soon, of course. Edwin had said that he might be meeting her. There was nothing suspicious in his walking here in the woods.

"It seemed to me I startled you the other evening," he said.

"The other evening?" She must force herself to speak naturally.

"Yes, on your way out to Terry's. You got to walking so fast that I sometimes almost had to run. I got terribly hot. Didn't you?"

"Yes," she said, "it was hot. Why were you following me?"

"Oh, it's a habit of mine."

She could imagine that he chuckled.

"There was nothing to be afraid of . . . then. I only wanted you to feel that I was there. That was all. Perfectly innocent. You feel that I'm here, don't you? You certainly must be feeling me here beside you. Because this is different. I'm glad you came to listen to my music. But that's not all there is. That's not the best."

She never could tell afterwards what it was: whether in the dark her eye made out a queer swift movement of his arm, or whether it was simply something in his voice; but before she knew it she had plunged through the bushes beside the road, rushing blindly on as she had done the other night after Harold; and Edwin was following her. She could hear his breathing now, heavy and desperate like a runner's on the point of exhaustion.

"No, no," he gasped. "No, no, you musn't go now. You can't go now."

She tried to scream and thought she succeeded in making a noise of some sort; and at that instant there came the crack of a revolver, and a violent tearing of leaves and branches.

"Daphne!"

It was Harold's voice. She stopped and leaned against a tree, her arms holding it closely so she would not fall to the ground.

"Daphne, it worked," he said. "I've got him!"

CHAPTER XIV

WHAT happened directly after that was always to remain somewhat confused in Daphne's mind. But in a few minutes not only Harold was there but Dave also; and then to her amazement she heard Paul Hatfield's voice. Then Harold was helping her into the front seat of Paul's car; Dave and Edwin, a silent collapsed figure, his hands bound behind him, were in the back; and after what seemed only a few minutes Harold and she were getting out in front of her apartment, and he was squeezing her arm as he led her upstairs.

When Harold turned on the lights and she looked about the familiar room, she could think clearly once more, but she sank down into her biggest armchair with a feeling of complete exhaustion.

"I'll get you a drink." Harold suggested, and presently he came back from the kitchen with two small glasses of whisky which looked almost neat.

"I need one myself," he said.

She noticed that his face though pale was dripping with sweat. There was a scratch on his cheek, and his yellow hair was rumpled over his forehead.

He raised his glass in her direction.

"Here's to you!" he exclaimed. "You know, dearest, I'm only just beginning to realize how close—how very close—we are to each other. I'm sure I experienced every instant of your terror—because it must have been terror—as you walked along that road. When Edwin appeared, I thought I could hardly stand it. I kept wondering how long he could hold off, when he would spring. I kept thinking he might reach you with his knife, that I might find you bleeding."

With a jerky motion he lifted his glass and gulped down the rest of his whisky. His lips and shoulders trembled as if from the burning liquor; then he gave her a swift sharp smile.

"That's better," he said. "Do you feel all right now?"

She had taken a few sips of her drink. "I don't know," she said. "I've no idea how I feel. I simply can't realize that it's over."

"At any rate, Edwin is caught."

"That's what I mean. What have they done with him, Harold?"

"Dave and Paul were going to take him right along to Brookfield. That's the state asylum. It's only ten miles from here. I got him in the thigh, and they can look out for it there, while they couldn't in jail. Of course he may have to be moved to prison and stand trial, but I doubt it. You can't try a man who is admittedly insane, and I don't believe there will be much question in Edwin's case. I imagine he'll never leave Brookfield. Yes, the danger from Edwin is certainly over."

117

"Is there any other danger?" she asked, struck by the oddness of his tone.

"Perhaps not," he said. "Let's not talk of it tonight. There is certainly none tonight. It's hard for me to think clearly at the moment. It's been a great strain, a great excitement. I feel very tired. I keep thinking of Edwin. It's awful, isn't it?"

"Yes," she said, and shuddered. For the first time she considered what this would mean for him. "To spend the rest of your life in an asylum! And I suppose he'll realize it. I suppose that his mind will be quite clear and normal on most subjects."

"Clear, perhaps. I'm beginning more and more to wonder what is meant by normal."

"But he'll be well treated, won't he? You read about strait jackets and brutal guards and solitary confinement."

"I imagine that at Brookfield he'll be treated in a civilized way, though I admit I have a phobia on insane asylums. I always have had since I was a boy. I've tried to break myself of it. But even if he were treated roughly, that would not be the worst thing. Far from it!"

"You mean the feeling that he could never be free again?"

"I mean that he'll never be able to kill again. He will never have another moment of complete rest or peace as long as he lives. That will be the real torture."

The next morning at ten o'clock, as she was finishing breakfast with Mary and Gerty, there was a knock at the hall door. Mary went to answer it and came back followed by Dave.

Daphne was delighted to see him. Ever since she had awakened an hour ago she kept having to remind herself that the mystery was solved, that Edwin was safely guarded; and yet she didn't have the sense of relief that she had imagined. It was as if her fear persisted, although there was no longer any need for it, just as the ground still seems to rise and fall under your feet when you step ashore after an ocean voyage. She did not exactly recall what Harold had said to her last night: she had been so tired, and Harold too had seemed quite exhausted, hardly his natural self; but she did remember that their talk had somehow not been

118

very satisfactory. There had not been the sense of a definite conclusion, a sudden change of key, the desperate hope for which had alone given her the strength to go through with Harold's scheme.

But the very sight of Dave was reassuring. Brown and brisk and smiling, he seemed to bring all outdoors into the apartment. Gerty offered him coffee, which he refused; and Daphne could see that he was just as eager as she was to get out somewhere where they could really talk to each other.

"You look pale," he said, "and no wonder! I think you need a walk. I can't offer you sunlight, but there's a nice breeze by the lake. I think we ought to catch it before it dies down."

It had rained a little during the early morning; the air was fresher than yesterday, and the sky was covered with low soft clouds. As usual on Sundays there were many canoes on the lake, and Dave suggested that they should get one themselves from the university boathouse.

"I don't think we better this morning," Daphne said. "I don't believe I told you that Wanda Hatfield made up some story to Harold about our picnic. She must have seen us from her lawn. I hope you don't like her, Dave. She told me you were a *very* good friend of hers, but I don't know anyone I dislike more."

He laughed. "Does the deer like the hunter?" he asked. "That may sound conceited, but with poor old Wanda every man is a deer. I didn't mean that terrible pun, by the way. Did Harold raise any objections?"

"I don't think he liked it. It was foolish of me not to tell him before Wanda got in her lick, but I just didn't seem to find the right opportunity. Harold was most reasonable, though."

"I can see his point," Dave said. "In fact I can see it very well. If I was your fiancée, I'd be jealous as hell if you went off for the day with another man. Even though I'm not your fiancée, I'm jealous, jealous as an old tomcat, of Harold. And let me tell you now, Daphne, that may have been why I was so damn disagreeable the other morning. I'll have to hand it to him. His idea worked, after all. I

119

still think it was outrageous, but it worked."

"How did you happen to be there?" she asked. "I've been wondering. And Paul too. Was it planned between all three of you?"

"No, that's the funny part," he said. "We were all there independently. I made up my mind that I'd do a little shadowing in my leisure time. I saw you starting out with Harold, and when I saw where you seemed to be going, I had a hunch he might be planning to spring something last night. So I just waited."

"You waited in the woods all evening!" she exclaimed.

"Sure. I had plenty to think about. And Paul tells me that he suspected something might be up. He didn't know exactly what; he was rather mysterious. But he was pleased as Punch to be in at the kill."

"It wasn't quite that," Daphne said. "Luckily for me! but tell me, Dave . . ."

She looked over the soft gray lake; the reeds and the water were both faintly rippled; a white gull was perched on a half-submerged log; and she wished she could feel the quiet peacefulness of the scene.

"Yes?" he said, and she realized that she had paused for a long time.

"It's hard to remember exactly what Harold said last night. We were both pretty much all in. But unless I'm just dreaming it, he did say something about there still being danger. How could that be?"

"I'll be damned if I see how!" Dave said. "But Daphne, I think I ought to tell you, in fact that's one of the reasons I came this morning: after we had left Edwin at the asylum, I said 'Thank God that's over!' or something of the sort. And Paul said: 'Over! I think you'll find it's just off to a good start!' You know the quiet way he has of talking. Of course I asked him what on earth he meant, but he wouldn't say. He sort of clucked mysteriously, and said he'd learned years ago not to stick his neck out. I let you have it for what it's worth."

For a moment, almost like an hallucination, Daphne saw the parched dim forest of her dreams; or were its twisted corridors the convolutions of a brain? It was filled with an

120

ironic silence, the silence of breathless waiting; and all at once the picture vanished, and she found herself remembering word for word a sentence she had read some weeks ago: "It's not unusual in cases of pulmonary tuberculosis for patients to be suddenly convinced they are on the road to recovery when actually the disease is entering its last and fatal stages."

She clutched Dave's arm.

"Do you suppose," she said with an effort, "that they think now that the others were not Edwin? But that doesn't make sense, Dave. Harold's whole point has been that it was all the same person. I don't think I could stand much more. I really don't."

"Damn it!" Dave muttered between his teeth. "Damn it! But I had to tell you, Daphne. Come along! Why don't you marry me, and we'll get out of here?"

She let go of his arm.

"Oh Dave," she exclaimed desperately, "why do you talk like that when you know I'm so upset, when you know I count on you so much? But how can I if you say such things?"

"All right," Dave said gruffly. "Forget it. At least for the present."

Harold had said he would come for her to take her out to lunch, but a few minutes after she reached home he telephoned her. "I'm sorry," he said, "but I drove out to Brookfield this morning and I feel pretty much all in just now. Do you mind if I don't come to lunch? I'll be there surely for dinner."

"But Harold, do you think you ought to come tonight? You didn't seem well yesterday evening, but I thought it was just the excitement and the letdown afterwards."

"That's all it is," he said, "but it's quite a letdown. I'll be fine tonight, though."

"How was Edwin?" she asked hesitantly. "Will they be keeping him there?"

"I'm sure they will," he said. "Poor Edwin has collapsed. A whole group of symptoms have developed. You'll be happier if I don't go into details, but there isn't the slightest doubt that he's legally insane."

She shuddered as she remembered Edwin's voice while he walked beside her in the darkness: no, that was not the voice of a sane human being.

"We had better eat here at home," she said, with an effort not to think of Edwin. "Is it cool enough for spaghetti?"

"Of course," he said. "Cool enough for anything! It's strange what a few degrees of temperature can make."

Daphne ate alone at the Union. She was sorry now that she had let Dave go, and would have called him up and suggested his having tea with her, if he hadn't asked her to marry him. She must be doubly careful after this never to thrust herself upon him.

That afternoon she took a long troubled nap. Most of the time she was only half asleep but she did not fully rouse herself until nearly six o'clock, and even then she felt good for nothing. Harold arrived as she was making the sauce for the spaghetti, and she found herself looking forward so eagerly to the cocktails that she decided in advance not to take more than one.

It was not until after dinner, as they sat together in the living room drinking coffee, that she put to him the question she had at once been dreading and longing to ask.

"Harold," she said, "last night you spoke as if there might still be danger. What did you mean?"

For a long time he did not answer and she watched him drawing hard at his cigarette. It occurred to her that she ought to urge him to stop smoking so much: he was now almost never without a cigarette between his lips.

"I don't remember speaking of it last night," he said finally, "but I'm glad you brought it up, because it's true."

"Perhaps you didn't," she said. "Perhaps I just imagined it; but I know Paul Hatfield thinks so."

"Paul!" He gave her a swift, almost startled look. "How do you know that?"

"Dave told me that Paul mentioned it to him."

"You've seen Dave since last night?"

"I went walking with him this morning. You don't mind, do you, Harold? I thought when we decided to be engaged we were both to be quite free to see whomever we liked."

"Are you particularly interested in Dave?"

122 ·

"I like him very much, don't you?"

"I don't trust him," Harold said in a low fierce voice. "I don't think you should trust him. But did he say why Paul thought there was still danger abroad? Was it danger for you personally?"

"Paul wouldn't explain. But mightn't it be the same thing that you had in mind?"

"Perhaps," Harold said. "It might be. It doesn't make much difference."

"But what *is* it?" Daphne asked. "I've been wondering about it off and on all day. Has something happened that makes you think it wasn't Edwin who committed the murder and attacked Margaret Peterson?"

"Of course it was Edwin," he said. "At least there is every reason to assume it was. No, the danger is something quite different. Wait a second while I mix myself a highball. Would you like one?"

"No thanks."

While she waited in the silent room, she noticed that it had begun to rain again very gently. She leaned back and rested her head upon the high pillow behind her; the lamp cast on the ceiling a circle of light which touched one of the corners by the window; and she saw suddenly that what she had thought was a small unexplainable shadow was a cobweb reaching from wall to wall. She looked quickly down at the magazines, the photograph of her mother, all the reassuring familiar things on the table beside her.

"I think I will have a highball," she said to Harold in the kitchen, "but make it a very weak one."

In a minute he returned with their drinks, and settled himself once more close beside her.

"Do you remember," he asked abruptly, "that the first time we dined at Terry's and we all were talking about the murder, I referred to the power of suggestion on an unbalanced mind?"

"I think so," she said. "I remember someone spoke of it, but there was so much talk about murder and famous murderers that I don't recall who said what."

"Anyone might have said it," Harold went on, "but as a matter of fact it was I. We've just had here in Woodside a sensational case. Edwin succeeded in committing one murder. and tried to commit two others of a very special kind. Very special, yes, and also on the whole very rare, surprisingly rare, it seems to me, unless there are some that escape detection . . . the bodies that are found. for example, floating in lakes or ponds. unrecognizable after months perhaps. the trunk murders you sometimes hear of, the people who simply disappear. Very special, and yet such murders are the result, as I've said before, of an instinct that exists to some degree in all of us, even if we are not aware of it."

"But Harold," she cut in hurriedly, "you said just the other day that it would be an extraordinary coincidence if two of the people at Terry's that night should both happen to have such a strong tendency toward sadism as to lead them to actual murder. And wouldn't it still be a strange coincidence if two people even in the whole of Woodside should prove to be such murderers? Because I think that's what you're driving at, isn't it?"

"You don't get my point," he said sharply. "Or rather you haven't let me make it. Of course it would be a coincidence if two people should develop in that way each one independently of the other. But in a town of this size, and I still insist especially in a college town, there are many high-strung people. Whatever you may think of the efficiency of professors in public life, the fact remains that their I.Q.'s are exceptionally high as a group; and when you find exceptional intelligence you may often find lack of stability. Many people have been following this affair with the deepest interest. For some, who knows, it may have been the acting out in real flesh-and-blood terms of the fantasies which for years have obsessed their minds—or perhaps merely the translation into waking life of what they have been wrestling with, hidden beneath a cloak of symbols, in their most secret dreams. And how can any one of us know when he wakes up, what he may have dreamed, for most dreams are forgotten? All our myths, all our religions are full of blood sacrifice—Abraham ready to kill Isaac, his own son; Agamemnon surrendering Iphigenia, his beloved daughter. The gods demanded it, they said. What were those gods? The deep urge that turned them against the

ones they loved, or rather that drew them irresistibly together, because by that sacrifice to a bloodthirsty god they
must have felt they reached a deeper, a more intense com-
munion than would have been possible in any other way.
You read of something happening a thousand years ago, or
happening in China, and even then it may be the kind of
thing that stirs your imagination; but how infinitely
stronger is the effect of something happening here and now,
something that has actually brushed you by! And surely
everyone here in town must feel he has been rubbing
shoulders with murder."

His voice had been so intense that it seemed still to echo
in the room.

"But Harold," she said after a minute, "I can't believe
that . . ."

"You can't believe? . . ." His tone had become almost
harsh. "Haven't you noticed again and again how crimes
come in waves, even the most banal crimes? And this is no
ordinary crime. From the point of view of the criminal it
is no crime at all; it is merely the following of an irresistible compulsion, achieving at least for the time the feeling
of peace, of rest, without which life is unbearable. There are
many examples of one such exploit releasing others which
without it might never have developed into the final stage
of action. In the winter of 1819-1820 there was a real epi-
demic of what they called *piqueurs* in Paris, men who
prowled the streets at night, stabbing women. Do you think
there actually were more potential sadists then than at any
other period? Of course not. One such stabbing occurred;
it stirred the mind of some other susceptible man, perhaps
someone who had even stumbled on the first attempt; and
presently from one to the other it spread through the city.
How did the legends of the werewolf and the vampire develop? Surely from the observation of such killings. And it's
easy to understand why certain regions got the dark reputation of being especially haunted by vampires or werewolves,
that the reputation sometimes lingered, and no doubt with
good reason, for centuries. In Liberia today there is a
dreaded secret society whose members are called leopard-
men, because they have developed the same tastes as the

125

leopard. No, it doesn't take very much to upset even the most normal mind, and when there is a jolt such as we have had here . . ."

He reached forward to throw his cigarette into the fireplace, and immediately lit another. When he spoke again his voice had lost its intensity, and sounded rather tired.

"Perhaps you see now, Daphne . . ."

"But you mean you think that someone else—anyone else —may continue these attacks?" she asked, still incredulous. "Of course I see what you mean. I can realize that it would be more likely to happen now. But you think it's likely enough, Harold? . . ."

And then such a terrible idea occurred to her that she drew in her breath sharply. "Do you mean you think that if it should happen again, the chances are that I would still be the one?"

"Yes," he said, "that's exactly what I mean."

Then, as if summoned from the depths of her mind to fight this horror, a wave of disbelief swept over her. "But the chances seem so slight, Harold, and unless you have some special reason . . ."

"I do have a special reason."

She fumbled for a cigarette, until he reached into the little enamel box and handed her one.

"What is it, Harold? You must tell me."

"I can tell you nothing more," he said. "I didn't mean to say what I have. It would be of no help, and I hope I'm wrong. I couldn't point out to you any one person. If I could, of course I would. My reasons are what you would dismiss as 'merely psychological.'" For an instant he smiled dryly. "But I do urge this: be distrustful of everyone. Daphne. No matter who it is. Take no one for granted. Don't go on any more picnics across the lake, for example."

"Harold, I won't believe that Dave . . ."

"You go with Dave at your own risk," he said with a sudden edge to his voice. "But I'm not merely warning you against Dave. I'm warning you against everyone, at least every man."

"Do you mean someone like Paul . . . or Terry . . . someone I know, or . . . just anyone?"

126

"I mean precisely what I say."

"Then you think I should keep on sleeping in the other apartment?"

He took a deep drag on his cigarette before he answered her.

"Yes," he said, "I do."

"But Harold, how long will this keep up? I don't know how long I can stand it."

This time he did not answer for at least a minute. Listening to the quiet rain, she remembered night before last, and the knocking at this door. Perhaps, after all, it had not been Edwin . . . but some nameless dark visitor as old as the human race.

"I don't know how long it will be," he said finally. "Perhaps until the end of summer. Perhaps, who knows, when the cool weather comes . . ."

He passed his hand over his face with a nervous tired gesture.

"I must be going now," he said, and got up from the divan. In the doorway, after he had kissed her good night, he turned and stared for a long moment deep into her eyes.

"Daphne," he said in a strange low voice, "you'll always remember that I warned you?"

CHAPTER XV

*T*HE next morning dawned hot and lifeless after the rain, and began what was to be the worst heat wave of the summer. An iridescent haze trembled over the woodlands, and the air seethed and flowed like molten glass along the glaring cement highways. In the victory gardens on the edges of town tomato plants hung limp from their stakes; the leaves of the cucumber and squash looked like wads of gray blotting paper. Dogs lay panting on their sides with feet extended, and the postmen as they went their rounds, their shirts dark with sweat, noticed that even the ones most apt to bark did not bother to glance at them or pull in their quivering pink tongues.

By the fourth day you could notice through the town a

127

faint disquieting smell from the lake which some said was merely due to the algae but which others suggested might be pollution. Occasionally at night the sky would cloud over; lightning would flicker on the horizon like the flaring of a distant barrage, and once or twice there was even a growl of thunder; but although there were a few showers about the country not a drop fell on Woodside. Night and day the air throbbed with the grating chirp of crickets and cicadas.

For Daphne this was a period of almost uninterrupted nightmare. Although she saw Harold every evening and often at other times, he did not stay with her as long as usual: he was very busy, he told her, at his office, working out some new visual tests. She did not know whether he had been a second time to see Edwin, and he did not speak to her again of danger. After the first day or so she felt that a convention of silence had been established between them.

But his manner hardly let her forget it: he had never seemed so restless, so distracted. He talked and even smiled more than usual, but his smiling seemed forced and did not alter the uneasy expression of his eyes. In the midst of his conversation his face would occasionally twitch (she had noticed this before, but only when he was very tired), and she knew he must be under great tension, that he must be as anxious, as tormented, as she was herself. They went several times to the movies and always chose the one theater in town that was air-cooled, irrespective of the program. It did not make any difference, because certainly she at least could never keep her attention on the picture, and she doubted if he could. But Harold did not like to walk in the heat, and it was pleasanter than sitting at home in her air-less rooms, where his constant fidgeting made her sometimes feel that she would cry out in sheer nervousness. She knew that he was worrying about her and trying not to show it; she knew that he was overworked; she knew only too well how the heat sapped one's energy and made sound sleep impossible.

She felt sorrier than ever for the people in the wards where she worked, especially for the ones in plaster casts. All the usual hospital smells seemed heavier, more penetrating; the patients who were not listless were apt to be ill-

128

tempered and unreasonable and she found that it was very hard not to answer them crossly.

But the exhausting thing wherever she might be was the feeling that she must always be on guard, that she must suspect everyone, that she was groping blindfold along the edge of a precipice. She recalled again her childish fear of leprosy, and now as she walked through the wilted sweating crowds she had the instinct to pull away from contacts, to keep glancing over her shoulder, as if the whole town had been mysteriously changed overnight into a leper colony . . . or a madhouse.

If she had not been so anxious about Harold, if she had not felt that she must look out for him more than ever, she might have given up her work at the hospital and left town. But where would she go? Barbara and her husband were living in one small room in Quantico which was crowded to overflowing; Jimmy was in the South Seas, and she had no friends whom she could bear to visit in her present state of mind. And more and more she began to admit to herself that there was another reason: the one friend, apart from Harold, whom she depended on now was Dave. The hour that she saw him, in the afternoon when her work at the hospital was done, was the consoling spot of her day; and the fear, the exhaustion, the confusion which she felt most of the time seemed to give to her talks with him, her strolls along the lake, a special brightness and security.

She realized, it is true, that Dave was the one person Harold had been willing to name in his strange passionate warning, and forced herself to remember that on their picnic across the lake Dave had produced his knife just before the boys had come up; but if the world had grown so mad that Dave might turn into a werewolf or a vampire, then she really did not care what happened.

On Sunday morning, just a week and a day after Edwin had been taken to the asylum, Harold came to her apartment as she was washing her breakfast dishes. It surprised her, because they had arranged the night before that he would come in the late afternoon to take her to dinner somewhere, and he had spoken of working in his laboratory most of the day. She had accepted, therefore, rather guiltily

129

Dave's invitation to lunch; and he had even tried to persuade her to cross the lake again and picnic at the spring.

Harold flung himself on the divan. His hair hung in sticky locks over his forehead, and she noticed that in spite of the heat he was wearing the same green shirt he had worn for the last four days. During this summer he had grown more and more careless about his clothes.

"I thought you were going to be working at your office," she said, wondering uneasily what he would say when he knew about Dave.

"It was a regular furnace!" he exclaimed. "It hadn't cooled off a bit overnight. And those rooms in Science Hall are so damn depressing I just couldn't stand it. I guess you've got me for all day."

"I wish I'd known," Daphne said, trying not to sound apologetic, "but Harold darling, Dave asked me to lunch with him, and I don't exactly like to back out now."

"Dave!" He made a sound between a grunt and a chuckle. "I bet you don't. Dave seems to be always popping up, isn't he?"

His tone irritated her.

"He's quite free to come when he wants to," she said, "but as a matter of fact he has been here very seldom."

Harold's face twitched. He sat up suddenly.

"I suppose you prefer to see him where you're less likely to be interrupted," he said.

She looked at him in surprise. "Harold," she asked, "what's got into you?"

He passed his hand across his face as if he were brushing away cobwebs.

"What's got into everyone?" he exclaimed. "What's got into me? What's got into you? What's got into Edwin? Ah, my girl, that we shall never know. We're all puppets, but who pulls the strings? That poor man in those pictures, did I ever tell you about him—the one in white, the one that lost the game to the one in black? He was really the devil, you know, and there was the devil to pay. I always used to think that I was the one in white. I used to blame myself. I used to be near despair. But what the hell, the cards were stacked!"

"You mean the pictures in your grandfather's house?" she asked. "The ones that used to hang on the stairs? I've thought of them often, and I've thought of you as a poor little boy going up to bed and not daring to look at them."

"But all that doesn't alter the fact that you've changed," he went on in sudden excitement. "That's all right, too, but it's irritating that you don't seem to think that I see it. After all, I'm not blind. A man can be driven just so far. You've got me, you know you've got me, and so you probably take a delight in trampling on me. It's only human."

"Harold darling, what do you mean? How have I changed?"

She went over to him quickly, sat down beside him, and put her hand on his knee.

He pushed it off with a swift gesture, stood up, and began pacing the room.

"Don't lie," he said in a strained voice. "A woman seems to think that if she touches your knee with her hand that's all she has to do and you'll believe anything. I suppose you love to touch Dave like that!"

"Harold," she said fiercely, "I won't listen to such talk! You ought to be ashamed of yourself. You act almost as if you were drunk. But then there would be some excuse."

"Drunk!" he exclaimed. "Not yet. A touch on the knee doesn't make me drunk. No doubt it does have that effect on Dave. I can just see him bending over your neck!"

As Daphne stared up at him she felt that all the sultry heat of these last awful days had set her brain on fire.

"Get out!" she ordered. "Get out of here, and don't come back until you can be decent!"

He stared at her an instant almost as if he had not understood. Then he flung himself on his knees in front of her and buried his head in her lap. His shoulders were shaken by long tearing sobs.

She was so startled, so amazed, that all her anger left her; then as she looked down at his tousled head, his quivering body, she was overcome with pity.

"Harold," she said gently, "Harold, darling, you mustn't! It's just that we're both on edge. It's the heat. It's the strain of the whole awful business with Edwin. And you had all

131

the responsibility, Harold. You were the one that made it come out all right. It was a triumph for you."

"Don't," he said at last in a half-choked voice. "Don't heap coals of fire upon me! How can you bear to look at me or have me near you? Why should you have been cursed with a man like me? If only I had never seen you, Daphne! Because then I was helpless. I'd never seen anyone like you. You were the angel, the Madonna, and for me even to look at you was a profanation. Will you ever be able to forgive me, Daphne? I wonder."

"Yes, yes," she said, "of course I will, Harold," and for several minutes she stroked his hair while his body grew more and more relaxed.

When at last he raised his head she smiled at him affectionately, and his answering smile, like the smile of a little boy, had such innocence and charm that she bent over and kissed him.

"I'll be going now," he said as he rose to his feet. "I won't bother you any more. Have a pleasant time with Dave. But you will let me come tonight, won't you?"

His tone was so humbled that she almost laughed: it reminded her of a repentant child asking his mother to look into his room before she went to bed. It occurred to her that perhaps she could even tell him that he should change his shirt, but she didn't quite dare.

"Of course you can come," she said. "I'll be counting on it."

She was dusting the living room when Dave arrived an hour later. He looked so brisk and shipshape after poor Harold, his smile was so brilliant, that for a moment she saw him as he had appeared to her the first time, at Terry Macfarlane's: the too perfect young man on the silver screen.

"I've got a neat lunch," he said. "What about our going to the spring? It's the coolest place I know of, and I suggest we wear our bathing suits. The water's not much more than a yard deep but even on a morning like this it will take your breath away."

Daphne hesitated. She did not want to worry Harold,
132

and yet when he left her just now he had been so meek and understanding. The best thing was probably to take him at his word, and if their stormy scene had cleared the air it might be just as well that it had happened. Besides, the temptation to escape from the town, to plunge into cold clean water, was irresistible. She had not swum in the lake for a month, because over here the water was so warm and dirty.

"All right," she said doubtfully. "Yes, I suppose we might."

"Swell!" He lifted his knapsack over his head. "Do you mind if I change into my trunks in the bathroom? I didn't dare come in them, because I was afraid you might think I was taking too much for granted."

Daphne went into her bedroom and slipped off her clothes which already were beginning to feel a little sticky. Her neat black bathing suit would be far more comfortable, and she was sure she was brown enough to escape a bad burn.

As Dave pushed off from the university pier, she remembered that the last time they canoed was the morning after Edwin—or was it Edwin?—had climbed into the tree outside her window. In spite of that she had begun to feel almost gay as the town had dwindled to a line of trees and buildings between lake and sky. But this morning she had no such lift. It was not, however, now so much dread that she felt as depression. She could not help thinking of what Harold had said, and although he had been excited and overstrained, she admitted that at least part of it was true: she had changed. She had never been fonder of him than when he looked up to her so humbly with tears in his eyes, and yet she knew that she was no longer in love with him. She even began to wonder if she ever had been. He had come to her when she was unbearably lonely, had touched her by his kindness, had dazzled her by his intelligence, but if even then she had really loved him why had she shrunk from the idea of marriage? Yet now when he was so disturbed, when he had grown to depend on her so completely, how could she bear to leave him?

She stared down into the water as it glided past them. It was filled with slimy green and brown particles, like the

133

water in a vase in which flowers have been kept too long; its surface was so smooth that if it had not been for the ripples from their boat, it might have been a turbid greenish jelly. But when she raised her eyes and looked back at the town—the pink and gray buildings peering from the trees, the chimneys, the steeples, the high-shouldered bulk of Science Hall, the lake became invisible as water and was merely the shore line upside down, with a few other canoes slipping languidly across it; and their own canoe was always just escaping the lower rim of the inverted sky.

It was a sky that was cloudless and yet nearer gray than blue, as if the mass of heat were slightly opaque, or as if the taint of decay were veiling the sun with a miasmatic film.

"You look sad," Dave said after a long silence, "or does the sun make your head ache? You should have brought a hat."

"No," she said, "it's not the sun. I guess I just feel tired."

"And afraid?"

"I seem to be always afraid. I've grown used to it."

"But not today," he said earnestly. "Forget it today. As a matter of fact, I'm beginning to think more and more that this talk of further risk is simply Paul's imagination and Harold's. You know how they both love to dwell on horrors."

She smiled at him because he sat so straight and looked so confident; she felt that if he were always beside her she would not be afraid.

"I won't be afraid today," she said. "It's horrid of me to slump down here like a cowed rabbit. Perhaps it *is* their imagination. I seem to have reached a point where it's hard to tell just where reality stops and imagination begins. You're not a werewolf, Dave, by any chance?"

"A werewolf?"

He flung back his head and laughed. As she saw his keen sharp teeth, his black lashes half closed over his clear bright eyes, she felt that if he should turn into an actual wolf, it would be such a sleek frolicsome animal, so friendly, so faithful, that she would love to run her hand through its fur. For the first time this morning she had caught his

134

mood, and knew that the day, after all, might be happy.

The canoe was passing now between the colonies of cow lilies, their leaves shredded and blackened at the edges, with lumps of brown stuff like rotten bark floating between them. Turtles were sunning themselves on water-soaked logs along the shore. The chirp and hum and buzz of insects grew louder.

"I've brought some citronella," Dave said, "in case there are mosquitoes, but I don't think there will be. That's one advantage of a dry summer."

More goldenrod was in bloom now along the banks of the stream, and Daphne exclaimed as she saw flaming among some tufts of sedge a clump of cardinal flowers. Dave nosed the canoe into the soft bank, balanced himself as he stepped among the slippery bunches of sedge, and picked her a few sprays.

"But they'll wither before we can ever get them home," she said.

"That may be, but you can have them for a little while. And when we've drunk our cocktails we can fill the bottle with water and stick them in it as a centerpiece. Just at present I feel very festive."

Although Daphne had been prepared for it, it was a surprise to feel the freshness of the air in the grassy spot around the spring; and when she dipped into the cold clear water she felt as if there might once again be cool free spaces in her mind. As they drank their cocktails, they sat on the bank with their feet still in the spring. Today Dave did not make a fire; he had brought hard-boiled eggs and cuts of sausage, peaches and small frosted cakes.

By the time they had finished dessert the water about their ankles had made Daphne feel so cool that she looked forward to the hot coffee in the other thermos bottle. Dave and she moved back from the edge of the water, and she watched him as he poured the black coffee into her tin cup. He glanced up at her; their eyes met unexpectedly, and with the bottle still in his hand he said: "Daphne, look here, you know I want to marry you. I told you so once and you shut me up. Well, I think a fair time has elapsed. I'm not going to try and say how much I love you. You're not dumb;

135

you can see it for yourself. What I want to know is, do you love me?"

He put down the thermos bottle on the grass; for a long minute she felt his eyes searching her face; and she knew that her impulse to make fun of him, to compare him to a movie star, an advertisement for tooth paste or for anything else, had always been pure defense. He was really the handsome, dashing, gracious person of whom the actors were only specious copies; and he was also kind and faithful and unassuming, which they did not even pretend to be. But all that was irrelevant.

He must have read her feelings in her face, because suddenly he had taken her in his arms and was kissing her mouth. "But Dave," she said in a few minutes, "what can I do about Harold?"

"You can break the news to him gently," he said. "What else? And I can't imagine anyone who would do it more kindly and sweetly than you would."

"But he depends on me so. And just now he's overwrought about Edwin. I can't just tell him brutally that I'm through with him."

"If *you* tell him, it won't be brutal. And there's no awful hurry, Daphne. Tell him as soon as you feel like it, as soon as you think it won't come as too much of a jolt. Of course it won't be easy. But you probably wouldn't want to marry both of us, even if the law allowed."

"And now, dearest," she said, and it gave her the greatest pleasure to think that it was Dave to whom she was speaking, "we must be getting back. You've got to change your clothes in my apartment, and I don't know when Harold may turn up. Poor Harold! The hard part is I think I'm fonder of him than ever."

"That's all right with me," he said. "Perhaps now I could even become fond of him too. But it would take some time."

The trip back across the lake seemed very quick. The air had cleared, and the town was glowing so softly in the afternoon light that even Science Hall, raspberry-colored against the blue sky, looked almost gracious. There were more canoes now than in the morning; and the gay bathing suits, the brown bodies of the students, had a subdued tropical brilliance. Again Daphne thought of her last picnic, and the dread she had felt returning: for the moment that seemed far away.

While Dave was putting on his clothes in the bathroom, the telephone rang. It was Harold.

"You're really coming out with me tonight, aren't you, Daphne?" he asked; and she was glad at least that his voice sounded cool and confident.

"Of course," she told him. "Did you think I wasn't?"

"No," he said. "I just wanted to make sure of you."

CHAPTER XVI

*A*S HAROLD walked down the stairs from Daphne's apartment that Sunday morning, he had felt for the moment that his tears had washed him clean. If he could only keep that feeling! He was awake now; he was himself. Most of the time he was neither waking nor sleeping: because if you could not sleep, you were never entirely awake; and it was in that dangerous border region that things stole up on you and got possession of you before you realized it. It was like sleepwalking; and he shivered as he recalled that twice during the last week he had waked up outside his bed. Once he had been opening the door that led to the stairs, and once he had been taking books from his bookcase.

Here is the smell of blood still. He had read that for the first time in high school; it was strange that they taught Shakespeare to students. *Macbeth* especially was so steeped in blood. And Baudelaire. . . . *La Fontaine de Sang,* the Fountain of Blood that stained all nature red. He remembered those curious red aphids that should have been green. Oddly enough that sonnet was not among the seven condemned poems. People simply did not understand.

But why should he worry? The very thought of blood, of violence, sickened him now, certainly more than it did the average person: it was like the aftertaste of some food which had poisoned you and which you could hardly think of without a recurrence of nausea.

137

"The fact is," he muttered, "that I've always been particularly squeamish. That's why I didn't study medicine."

He noticed that a student passing him had given him a curious glance and realized that he had spoken aloud. One of the most difficult things during the last week had been not to talk to himself in the presence of others. That was why he preferred on his walks to go out of town, even in the dead of the night.

Those walks of his! Almost every night, sooner or later, when his room became unbearable, he had dressed and gone out and walked through the sleeping town, the hot empty country. His thoughts had taken on the grinding rhythm of the cicadas, or throbbed with the pulsing of the stars, or sometimes escaped on quivering flights with the long-drawn hooting of the owls: they had been never still. That was why you couldn't stay in a room; you always had to be somewhere else. Each pause was merely provisional, until you caught your breath.

He remembered earlier in the summer chasing a bat which had somehow got into Daphne's room. He had driven it from one end to the other, flicking at it with a towel; it would alight for an instant on the top of a picture frame; it would fall behind the table, and as he struck at it it would again take flight, but a shorter, jerkier flight, until at last cornered on the floor, its teeth chattering with rage and terror, it had been covered by the towel and his fingers had closed about its struggling body.

But for himself, it was flight from what? Perhaps he would not have been sure even now, if it had not been for his half-remembered dreams.

Of course he was not sure. He was not doomed. That was an idea he must not admit. He was a free agent. Everyone was a free agent.

He wondered if Daphne and Dave would cross the lake. He might call up Wanda, because if they passed her garden they would be going in that direction, and she was jealous enough of Dave not to mind watching. "I'm not jealous," he muttered, "because obviously neither Dave nor Daphne is to blame. If they are pulled together, it has been specially manipulated to goad me on to my doom. But no, that's just

138

the way I must not allow myself to think. And it would be mad to call up Wanda."

At any rate he must lie down for a bit. Last night he had been out from one o'clock until nearly four.

When he reached his room he pulled down the shades and stretched himself on his bed without bothering to take off his clothes or wash the sweat from his face. The room was filled with an orange gloom, and as he stared at the ceiling he began to feel again the familiar pressure around his head. Is it something physical, he wondered, or do I just imagine it? The sensation is there. Is it the result of some organic change? That's what I mean. It's when I try to think consecutively that it seems to come. But it comes also when I make no effort not to think. I must make no effort.

His face tickled as if something were crawling over it, but he realized that it was only sweat. He closed his eyes. Again he saw his office in Science Hall, the big cluttered desk, the filing cabinets. The orange shades were drawn because it was night. Then he was carrying something up the stairs, surprised as usual because it was no heavier; he was walking, feeling his way, through the dissecting room, among the metal tanks, then through the low corridor beyond, with its row of little separate rooms, unwindowed, with the glimmer of the stars shining down through the skylights. In each of these rooms were one or two tanks with their pails under them, and in the last room of all there were three more, unused, waiting . . .

Even in this heat, it would be several days; and up there you were not so apt at first to notice strange odors.

Then he was coming down, floating lightly, serenely; he was going to sleep.

He made a violent effort; it was as if he were himself enclosed in one of those metal tanks. He could not move; he could not stir a finger; he was being pushed down, he must struggle back at any cost. This was the wrong kind of sleep!

The slightest movement anywhere would unlock his prison. He must stop, not think, relax, then try suddenly again. His mouth twitched. He opened his eyes. His clothes

139

were as drenched as if he had been under a shower. Why always that? he asked himself. Is it just because I've been working there so much . . . or trying to work? Or is it because the woods belong to Edwin?

He blinked several times, sat up with a jerk, and looked at his watch. Five minutes past eleven! He had only been lying here for about half an hour. If he were going to call Wanda, he had better do it quickly.

It was only when she answered him that he remembered he had decided he should not do this. Well, it was too late now. What difference?

"Wanda," he said, "I am going to ask you to do something that may seem rather odd, but I think you'll understand."

"That sounds thrilling!" she exclaimed. "I'm all ears."

"I think that Daphne and Dave may be picnicking across the lake again. I remember you saw them the last time, and it occurred to me that if you happened to cast an eye on the lake now and then you might notice them. But it's really of no importance."

"I was just going to put in a little gardening," she said. "If I see them I'll give you a ring, shall I?"

"Don't tell me that you actually garden yourself!" he exclaimed, pleased at his natural half-joking tone.

"Of course I do. I'm afraid you don't understand me, Harold. I'm really just a sweet home girl."

"Don't bother to call unless you feel like it. I'm just interested psychologically, nothing more."

"Sure, I get you. So long!"

The moment after he had hung up he tried to remember whether or not she had said she would actually call. He had got the idea that she would, but was that only his assumption? It annoyed him that he could not remember her literal words. He started toward the telephone; he would call again; but he stopped, with a twinge of fear, before his hand touched it: that would seem much too strange!

If they were going they should be starting very soon. He would wait around for awhile. But suppose they were not going; then Wanda would not call, and he would be waiting here for hours. That would be quite impossible. If he did not hear from her by noon, he would call her on some other pretext and mention the picnic incidentally, as if it did not matter, which of course it didn't.

He walked up and down the room. His head throbbed. There was nothing so dreary as waiting for a telephone call. He was smoking his fourth cigarette when the bell rang.

"Hullo, Harold," Wanda said. "They just went by. In their bathing suits, if that interests you. At least I assume Dave had his pants on. He wasn't wearing a top."

"Oh fine," he said. "Thanks a lot. As a matter of fact, I'd forgotten all about it, but thanks just the same. Goodby."

The pressure was again around his head, as the room turned slowly. Was it pushing him away from something, toward something? Toward that kind of waking half sleep, perhaps.

"I know what I should do," he said suddenly in his natural voice. "I should go and see Edwin again. That certainly should wake me up. That should be a salutary warning. Even better than those card players."

He noticed the state of his clothes. That was lucky: he must smell like a tramp; he certainly looked like one. He stripped himself where he was standing, leaving his clothes on the floor, went into the bathroom and stood under the cold shower until he began to shiver. "I'd hate to have the water cure," he thought with a flash of intense fear gone so quickly he hardly remembered it.

He dressed himself carefully, brushed his hair, and left the apartment. It would not be visiting hours at Brookfield, but Dr. Carey would let him in at any time. "The hard thing," he muttered with a dry laugh, "is to get out of those places." It was not until he was seated in his car and had pressed his foot on the starter that he saw he had forgotten to put on any socks.

"What the hell," he chuckled, "I'm just an absent-minded professor."

But as he turned into the driveway at Brookfield, so treacherously peaceful under its huge elms, he began to wish he had not come. He did not know whether he could force himself to enter the door of the long yellow brick building where the new patients were kept, and where Dr

141

Carey had his office. This was the test, perhaps. If he could surmount this, all would be well. It was good medicine. Better visit here for half an hour than for life!

He was actually trembling as he walked up the steps and was thankful that Dr. Carey happened to be in his room: if he had had to wait for long he might not have been able to keep up a decent appearance of calmness.

"Is it all right if I look in on Edwin Voigt?" he asked.

"Sure! Go right ahead, Professor. You're always welcome. I wish we saw you oftener."

Dr. Carey's voice was singularly deep; he looked like a rather sinister black-bearded Santa Claus. and the hair on his wrists was almost as thick as a gorilla's.

"Voigt is a stubborn little guy," he went on. "He won't talk and he'll hardly eat. I don't think he'd eat at all, if we hadn't started feeding him by a tube through his nostril."

As Harold followed the doctor along the main corridor with its rubber matting, its smooth gray walls, he could see men in dressing gowns padding to and fro on the sun porches at the ends of the side passages. Now and then from a distance he could hear a sharp command, a hum and a buzz of confused sound. Once, looking upward, he met the eyes of a yellow froglike face with no chin, peering down at him through a wrought-iron ventilator in the ceiling. The whole place smelled of phenol and stale cabbage.

Edwin lay in a cot in a little putty-colored room, with a single grated window. Dr. Carey left Harold at the door.

Edwin had changed in the week since Harold had seen him last. His sunken gray face made his eyes seem enormous, and his mustache looked like a piece of crude make-up for a melodrama. He glanced at Harold but did not speak and showed no sign of recognition.

"Hullo, Edwin," Harold said. "How are you?"

Though Edwin made no reply, Harold could imagine that his eyelids narrowed a shade into an expression of concentrated irony.

Harold stood by the foot of the bed and looked down at him for a minute: it was hard to think of anything to say that would not be the height of futility. Then as he stood

142

there he found himself trembling once more; he felt that at any cost he must keep it from Edwin. "There's a piano in the lounge," he said. "When you feel better you'll be able to play. I'll see that your music is sent out."

Perhaps the faintest smile moved Edwin's lips under his mustache. Harold could not be sure; but it was not a smile of pleasure or of friendliness.

Suddenly Harold clutched the iron bar at the foot of the cot and leaned forward over the sheet.

"Tell me," he asked in a quick low voice, after a glance toward the door. "that time with the girl, in the woods, when Daphne and I interrupted you, was it all for nothing, Edwin? Did we come too soon?"

He was terrified at his question because he had not meant to ask it: it was as if someone else had spoken, to trap him, to cut off his escape.

"Well," he said after a moment, "I must be going, Edwin. I'll be out here again."

Then for the first time Edwin's face quivered; and when he spoke it was startling, because his voice, in its dry malice. sounded so completely natural: "I know you will," he said. "I'm looking forward to it."

Harold left the room quickly; he was trembling so that his teeth knocked together. and it was all he could do to keep from running down the endless rubber-carpeted passage.

It was a little after four o'clock when he reached his own room. He did not remember exactly what he had done in the meantime, except that he had parked his car somewhere on a side road and got out. He must have walked, because his shoes and the bottoms of his trousers were dusty. Of course he had walked. He suddenly recalled that he had grown hungry and picked two tomatoes off a vine in a farmer's garden and a woman had shouted at him.

Speaking of hunger, he felt thirsty now, thirsty as the devil. He was pouring himself a shot of whisky when someone knocked at the door. His first impulse was not to open it, but what the hell, it might be Wanda with more news. It might even be Daphne!

143

As a matter of fact, it was Paul.

"Hulla, Harold," he said. "I'm lucky to find you at home at this time of day. Wanda and I had planned a picnic for tonight, with Terry and Jeanne, and we thought it would be pleasant if you and Daphne came along."

"Have a drink," Harold said. "I don't generally drink alone, but it was so damn hot, I was just succumbing."

"Thanks, I should like one," Paul said, and sat down.

"Daphne's off for the day," Harold said as he handed Paul his glass.

"Really? But she will be back in time, won't she?"

"Who knows?" Harold asked slyly. "But even if she is, we have a date for tonight, Paul. Thanks just as much."

"You better come along with us," Paul coaxed.

"No thanks. She's picnicking with Dave, you know. Perhaps Wanda told you. I have to get in my innings sometimes."

"Well, if you change your mind before six, let us know."

"Thanks, I will. And thank Wanda for me. She helped me quite a lot this morning."

Paul cocked his eye at him sharply.

"Oh that!" he said. "My dear Harold, if you really want the opinion of someone who knows her rather better than most, Wanda's a little devil, or would be if she had the intelligence. If you believe what she says, you're crazy!"

"That may be," Harold said, and heard his own wooden laugh.

As soon as Paul had gone, he felt overcome with sleep. Perhaps it was the whisky. He lay down cautiously on his bed, as if to steal a march on his thoughts, and the next thing he knew he was opening his eyes, jolted into wakefulness again by the shock of a persistent dream which had vanished entirely.

It could not have been a bad dream, though; quite the contrary, because his brain felt clear and light. The confusion and strain and worry of the last few days seemed very remote; it was even hard to remember it, now that everything was so simple. In so far as he did remember it, it was like the worry of another person.

He looked at his watch. Almost six. There was just one

144

thing: he must make absolutely sure of Daphne. She could not fail him, because tonight he was counting on a real sleep. There must be no dreams of any sort.

It was then that he went to the telephone and called her number.

CHAPTER XVII

*A*FTER Dave went, Daphne took a shower and put on a clean white dress. As she noticed the glowing brown of her face and arms against the fresh muslin, she found herself regretting that Dave would not be seeing her tonight. Then she was ashamed of her selfishness. Poor Harold, had she lost all interest in him because she was no longer in love with him? But she knew this was unfair: of course she wanted to look nice for Harold, but just now she could hardly think of anyone but Dave. She wondered whether she could tell Harold this evening. His voice had sounded so confident over the telephone that perhaps she could. But she would wait and see.

While she was brushing her hair there came a knock at the door. She gave it one more brush, and was pleased with the way it fluffed about her shoulders. She was sorry that she had not yet put on her lipstick and smiled to think that just now she had been conscience-stricken at not caring how she looked for Harold. "If I should worry about anything," she thought, "it should be my own vanity." But she knew that this too was unfair: it was merely because she felt that, unlike Barbara who couldn't be anything but beautiful, she must always look her best to be even attractive.

When she opened the door she was surprised and a little relieved to find it was not Harold but Gerty.

"How nice!" she exclaimed. "Come in! Harold will be here presently, and you must stay and have a drink with us before we go out."

Gerty stepped into the room, peering around through her thick glasses, her short hair hanging in rattails over her forehead. Daphne felt especially friendly toward her: she was really the kindest soul, and most intelligent; perhaps sometime it might be possible to give her a few suggestions about her clothes.

"I can't stay a minute." she said. "But I'm afraid I've done an awful thing. Daphne. Professor Hatfield telephoned about an hour ago and asked if I'd be sure and tell you to call him before half-past six, and it's quarter to seven now. Apparently he tried to get you several times and no one answered."

"I'm sure it doesn't make the slightest difference," Daphne said.

"But he told me it was important. You'd better try at once."

"All right. I will," Daphne said. "But if it's about anything for this evening, I'm busy anyway, so it won't matter. And if it's not, the morning will do just as well."

"You will call, though, right away? I feel so guilty."

"I'll call at once."

She was amused to see that Gerty lingered in the doorway until she had lifted up the telephone; then she went out, closing the door softly.

The line gave the busy signal, and Daphne went back to her dressing table.

Harold himself did not arrive until nearly half-past seven. In contrast to the last few days, he looked very neat. He wore no coat, but his duck trousers, with their rigid creases, were evidently just back from the laundry, and his shirt, open at the neck, looked as fresh and white as her own dress.

"How lovely you are, Daphne!" he exclaimed. "I was hoping you would wear white. You look like a bride!"

She felt that she blushed a little; it would certainly be very hard to tell him.

"You look handsome yourself," she said.

"Don't you recognize me?" he asked. "The figure in white."

"The figure in white?"

He smiled. "Don't tell me you've forgotten already. How short your memory is! The poor man in the picture. except that what he wore looked more like a monk's cowl."

146

She returned his smile with some constraint.

"The way you spoke of him, I always thought he must be terribly scared and wretched. If he was as brisk as you are now, I can't feel very sorry for him."

"Oh those pictures." he said airily, "they were just pictures, after all. Bugbears to frighten children. I remember when I was a kid and took piano lessons I had a little piece by Schumann, and that was the English translation of the title. *A Bugbear to Frighten Children.* I never was sure what a bugbear was, and I didn't like to ask. I always pictured it as a sort of huge spider with long fur on its back like a bear."

"Ugh!" Daphne exclaimed with a shiver. His mention of a spider had reminded her of Edwin; and she realized that for the first time in days she had been forgetting her fear. "That sounds horrible!"

"It wasn't real," he said. "It didn't exist!"

"And now," she suggested, "I suppose you'll be wanting a cocktail."

"As a matter of fact I don't," he answered. "I thought we would have some wine with dinner. Tonight I have a sort of hankering for wine—red wine. It will look very pretty with your white dress."

"I think it will be awfully nice," she said. "I love wine, but I didn't think you cared for it."

"It seems appropriate for some occasions. It has a long tradition behind it. What are cocktails? Pleasant, I admit, but no associations, no poetry. Do you know Baudelaire's little series of poems about wine, by the way? *Le Vin des Amants, Le Vin de l'Assassin* and so on?"

"Of course I don't," she said. "The only Baudelaire poems I ever read were in the anthology we had for French 21a."

"Too bad. But they wouldn't be apt to choose those. Well, shall we be off?"

At the door Daphne hesitated.

"I just remembered I was supposed to call up Paul Hatfield before half-past six. I tried once at quarter to seven, but the line was busy. Do you suppose it's worth trying again?"

"He came to see me this afternoon," Harold said. "He wanted us to go on a picnic with them and the Macfarlanes but I told him we had a very special engagement. Was that all right?"

Daphne could not help thinking, with a stab of regret, how much rather she would have gone on a picnic tonight with a group of people than spend the evening alone with Harold, but she must not let him see her disappointment.

"Of course," she said. "Where do you think we'll go?"

"I thought of the Chicken Shack," he said. "It would be pleasant if we could get one of the tables in the summerhouse where we were the other evening."

Daphne remembered that it was in that screened summerhouse that Harold had first suggested using her to trap Edwin. Until tonight she would have shrunk from going back there, but now she felt she would not mind, and it would be nice driving through the country.

It was after eight o'clock when they reached the Shack, and Daphne was faintly sorry to see that there was no one in the summerhouse: Harold and she would have it to themselves. However, she decided she would not speak of Dave until after dinner. Perhaps not even then.

Harold ordered a bottle of red Italian wine, and they sat for a long time in the thickening dusk, smoking cigarettes and sipping from their glasses. The moon hung above the rim of the woods across the road, a smoky yellow disk whose light seemed to preserve and concentrate the heat of the past day. Whippoorwills called mechanically; in the distance a dog barked.

"The dog days," Harold said. "Before long they will be over. Tonight must be full moon. It looks perfectly round, doesn't it? There are all kinds of superstitions about the time of the full moon. I wonder how many of them are based on fact."

"What are they?" she asked.

"Some of them are rather grim," he said. "We won't talk of them now."

When the chicken came, crisp from the frying pan, Harold turned on the light above the table, and moths began to knock and whir against the screens.

148

"What were you doing today?" Daphne asked. "Did you go back to your laboratory?"

"Yes," he told her. "I was there most of the day. The tests are coming along in pretty good shape. You might be interested in looking over them sometime."

"Exactly what are they, Harold? You never told me."

"They are a sort of variant on the Rohrschach tests. You know what *they* are, don't you?"

"Are those the ink blots?"

"That's how they started. Some of them now are in color. People interpret them differently, and from the pictures they see in them, I mean the general type of interpretation, you're supposed to be able to judge something about their minds, whether they have abnormal tendencies, and so forth."

"Do you believe in them?" she asked.

"Oh, they are all right as far as they go, but I've been trying to carry them a little further. I've been working with colors especially. I've been trying to reduce pattern to a minimum. It seems to me that the way people react to clots of pure color might be very revealing. Yes, sometime before long I'll run through my slides for you. But what have *you* been doing, Daphne?"

"Dave took me across the lake," she said. "We picnicked again. I'm afraid you'll scold me for going so far."

He smiled. "Not at all, as long as you came back. I was probably exaggerating when I spoke of danger. It's so easy to worry, especially when you're tired. It's so easy to imagine things. Did you have a good time?"

"Yes, I had a lovely time. We went bathing in the pond by the spring and felt really cool."

"I was sure you must have enjoyed yourself," he said, "because you looked so radiant and blooming when I opened the door. I could imagine you as the young Persephone, before she was carried off to hell. I'm glad you had a good time today, though—very glad."

Daphne gave him a surprised glance: his tone had not sounded sarcastic, and there was no sign of irony in his face.

She smiled at him gratefully. "That's very kind of you, Harold," she said.

149

"No," he said, "I'm not particularly kind."

"Oh but you are! I'll never forget how you looked after me in those weeks after Mother died. I don't know what I'd have done without you."

"It's curious," he said, "to wonder what would happen to people under different circumstances. What would have happened to you, for example, or to me, if we had never met? Would you like another bottle of wine?"

"Not for me. But you order one if you'd like."

"No, you're right," he said. "It is probably better not. A little wine heightens the sensibilities, but beyond that it dulls them. You remember the porter in *Macbeth*."

The moon was now so brilliant that they could see its light across the floor of the summerhouse. Harold glanced at his watch.

"Would you believe it!" he exclaimed. "It's nearly half-past ten. I suppose we might as well be starting home."

As they drove slowly along between the pale metallic fields and the checkered woods, Daphne kept trying to make up her mind to tell him about herself and Dave. If it was cruel to shatter his cheerfulness this evening, it seemed even worse to let him continue his illusion.

She had just keyed herself to the point of beginning, as they were approaching the lights of the town, when Harold spoke himself, and for the moment she had lost her chance.

"Daphne," he said, "You know what I'd like to do? I'd like to show you my tests. Let's stop in at the laboratory on the way home, and I'll run through some of the slides. It won't take long, and I'd be curious to get your reactions."

Daphne would have preferred to go straight home, but tonight of all nights the least she could do would be to show interest in Harold's work.

"I'd love to!" she exclaimed, and tried to sound enthusiastic. Perhaps she could tell him there; it might be easier than speaking of it as they drove through the streets.

He did not answer her and presently turned off College Street on to the thickly wooded campus. In the black and white moonlight it seemed to extend for miles in all directions, and she was surprised at how soon he drew up in the parking space behind the huge mass of Science Hall.

150

"We'll have to go round to the main door," he said. "That's the only one for which I have a key, and at this hour the doors will all be locked."

Their footsteps on the cement walk that skirted the building sounded very loud; it was as if the moon had extracted every bit of moisture from the air so that noises rang sharp and dry. The arched basement windows, with their copings of rough-hewn granite, made her think of a fortress or a dungeon. Their panes of plate glass reflected the moonlight blankly, but as she passed close by each one she could catch a glimpse through the reflection of a cavernous darkness within.

"I'm glad you're with me, Harold," she said. "This isn't cheerful at night, especially after what has been happening."

"You notice the peculiar shade of the bricks in the moonlight?" he asked. He reached over and stroked the wall with his fingers. "They still seem to be radiating warmth."

She was glad when they came around the corner to the front of the building, facing the street. The heavy arched doorway, with its polished granite pillars on either side reminded her of the box of cement blocks she had had as a small girl. They were German, and had been her father's. Most of them were brick-red oblongs of various sizes, but there were a few blue-gray cylinders and plinths; in a little booklet in German there were pictured, against wooded landscapes, the gateways and shrines and bridges that you could build with them; but these always looked somehow wrong, like objects in a bad fairy tale, because the individual blocks were so much too big compared with the whole construction and the surrounding trees.

Harold had some trouble unlocking the heavy door, but in a minute he pushed it part way open.

"Step in," he said. "Welcome to the temple. I'll take you presently to my holy of holies. You've never been to my office, have you? This will be your initiation—the night of the full moon! They used to believe it had some effect on the insane."

"I've never been in the building," she told him. "I had no classes here and it always seemed so oppressive."

"I must give you some light," he said, and touched a

151

switch to the right of the doorway that turned on a dim yellow bulb in the entrance hall. The ceiling was very high; the floor was of gray and blue tiles; and from inside, the place reminded her of a bleak railroad station. It looked at once strange and unpleasantly familiar. The iron stairway wound about the meshwork cage of an elevator.

"You're on the second floor, aren't you?" she asked.

"Yes, but I'm quite a distance from here, off in the north wing. This place is a labyrinth."

They walked side by side up the stairs, two flights really, because they were broken by a wide landing which passed behind the elevator shaft; and when they reached the second story he turned on a light at the end of a corridor, turned off the switch by the elevator, and led her past a row of closed doors, until he turned on still another switch and again put out the light behind him. Other corridors branched from the ones along which they walked, and now and then she would see a square of moonlight far away.

"They are always after us to be careful of the electricity," he explained. "War economy, you know."

By the time they stopped before one of the doors, Daphne had quite lost her sense of direction. These passages, all alike, were as confusing as the paths in a wood. Opposite the door a narrow stairway led up into the darkness above, and just beyond, down three or four steps, the same corridor kept on into the shadow, at a slightly lower level.

When Harold opened the door of the office and turned on the light inside, Daphne blinked at the glare.

"Welcome once more," he said. "Our journey is ended."

The office was a tiny yellow room with a large desk. The ceiling was so high in proportion to the size that the place made Daphne think of a cell in a honeycomb. Harold went around the desk and opened a door behind it.

"The laboratory is in here," he said, and switched on another light.

Daphne followed him curiously. This second room was large, with an enormous table down the center; there were colored charts on the walls, which seemed to be statistics of some sort; on a shelf were some cubes and prisms painted white; and in one corner what looked like a projector for

152

moving pictures was covered with a cloth. The room was intensely hot.

Harold went to the nearest window but instead of opening it as she had expected he pulled down the orange shade. Then he pulled down the shade of the other window.

"Don't you think it would be a good idea to open one of the windows?" she asked. "It's terribly close in here."

"They are not screened," he said, "and when you open them after dark with this bright light, all kinds of insects and moths come in. We won't be long now."

"But you will have to turn out the lights when you show the slides."

"It *is* hot! Perhaps we won't bother with the slides."

"If you held just a few up against the light," she suggested, "I could get an idea of them."

He smiled, and one end of his mouth was pulled downward by a sudden twitch. "As a matter of fact, Daphne, my love, there aren't any slides."

"There are not any slides?" She stared at him in amazement, thinking that she must have misunderstood.

"None that I've made, at least. They simply don't exist."

"Then why did you bring me here?"

She felt that in a minute she would be furiously angry, and she must not be angry with him a second time today. Unless, that is, she should use her anger as an excuse for breaking the engagement—but no, she felt that this would be deceitful and unworthy.

"Well, for one thing I wanted to talk to you."

A strangeness in his voice made her think that perhaps he already suspected.

"I've been wanting to talk to you," she said, trying to keep her temper. "There has been something I've been meaning to say all evening."

He held out his hand with a deprecating air.

"I think I can guess. It really makes no difference."

"I don't think you can, Harold. This is serious. What I wanted to tell you was . . ."

"That you and Dave have decided you love each other? It doesn't surprise me. And you always will have had one happy day."

The anger which she had been trying to control was drained from her. In spite of the heat she felt suddenly cold, and her heart seemed to swell so that she could not breathe. Harold was staring at her intently with an expression she could not understand, that she had never seen before: his face had become a primitive mask, expertly carved, but terrible, like a face in a dream. And these corridors . . .

"Harold," she said sharply, "what's the matter. Why did you bring me here?"

"I didn't want to be interrupted." His words were very clear though his lips hardly seemed to move.

"But why here? I hate it here! I want to go, Harold. I want to go at once."

"That's what I thought. You might have got frightened. You might have tried to run away."

"To run away? Why should I run away?"

"As you did from Edwin."

She drew in a choking breath. Here in this dry metal forest, it had caught up with her at last.

CHAPTER XVIII

THE room trembled as if it were dissolving in waves of heat. "I must not faint," she told herself. "If only I can keep from fainting!"

With a silent shock, the white light in the ceiling, the orange window shades, and Harold himself, standing between the windows, beyond the dull shine of the table, slid into focus.

Daphne tried to swallow but her mouth and throat felt as if she had been chewing ashes. "I'm sure you wouldn't do me any harm, Harold," she said at last.

"How can we measure harm?" he said. "Were you doing me harm when you let Dave make love to you? Of course not. I can see quite well now that it was not malice. Will I be doing you harm when I make you entirely my own—once and for all—in the slow, the inevitable torture of the final sacrifice? It was with joy, with ecstasy, that the Hindu widows flung themselves among the licking flames of the funeral pyre. The men they loved had already won their sleep, and surely you will not grudge it to me!"

She noticed that he had not moved any nearer. If only she could reach the door behind her! It would take him a moment to get around the table. If only she would not have to fumble at this door and the one from the office into the passage! But she felt that she was paralyzed, that Harold and she were irrevocably fixed in relation to each other, as if the air had thickened into a firm transparent jelly. It was pressing on her forehead, her temples, it was trying to force its way into her head and paralyze her brain. She must make herself keep thinking, planning.

"You probably will not feel that ecstasy," he went on with his strangely unmoving lips, "unless it is the ecstasy of terror. But that, you will find, is nearer the excitement of great joy than you had imagined. Just as you will find that pain is only the secret name for pleasure. There will be plenty of time. There is the whole night before us. Don't you see that there can be no true sacrifice, no complete consummation, unless the victim dies? And without complete consummation there can be no sleep. Don't you know that the heart—the heart dripping blood—is a symbol of both human and divine love, and only through such love can you win salvation and peace."

Had she been standing in this stifling room throughout eternity? How would she ever find her way among those passages? And even if she should reach those huge front doors, perhaps in this old building you needed, even from inside, the key to unlock them. But she would never reach those doors. She could see herself running through this black maze, and coming to a dead end where she would cower until a moment later this mask that was not Harold would turn on the light, and move toward her with the leisurely calm of complete certainty. What kind of knife would he carry? Would it be a long clasp knife like Dave's?

Dave! For an instant the room reeled again as hope, a desperate hope poured back into her veins. It could not yet be midnight, and Dave worked alone until all hours. His office was at the very top, under the roof, three stories above. There was a little stairway opposite the door. If

155

she could reach the turn and be out of sight, before Harold stepped into the hall, he would naturally suppose that she had run along the corridor to escape from the building!

The spell was broken. She knew that she could move her limbs. She could climb those stairs to find Dave; and even if she did not find his office, and it would be the barest chance if she did, she could scream until he heard her.

She turned, and the next instant felt the doorknob inside her hand; the door opened and she slammed it behind her. She fled around the desk in the tiny office; this other door must have a spring lock, because there was a small metal knob below the big one. Without calculating, she seized them both; the lock clicked; she pulled open this second door, slammed it as she had done the first, and ran up the little stairway into the darkness above. She had to pause on the small landing or her heart would burst; but she was around the curve, out of sight from below, and Harold was only now opening the door into the hallway.

He paused for a moment outside: she could hear his breathing. And only then she remembered that this was Sunday; it was not one of Dave's regular evenings to be here; there was still a chance but she could not know. Approaching the building from behind, she had not been able to see his window, and as they walked around to the front they were much too near to see any of the windows except those in the basement and a few on the main floor. She must control the pounding of her heart.

Then she heard his feet starting along the corridor in the direction from which they had come. She clutched at the banister in her relief, and the next instant, from close to her ear, there came a long quivering sigh. Harold's footfalls stopped. Then she heard them returning.

It had been her own sigh. She had given herself away!

She ran up the rest of the flight, and could see that it continued to the fourth story. Through the window slit on the landing she had caught a glimpse of the moonlit lake, and realized that Dave's office must at any rate be on this side of the building. She kept on upward, gasping now for breath, and hearing always the soft unhurried steps just a flight below her.

156

Those steps had been tracking her down since that evening three weeks ago when she had heard them first among the parched shadows of the wood. If they had sometimes seemed to pause, to give her time, it was just because they were so sure. It was because they were sure that they did not hurry now.

It had been Edwin then, and tonight it was Harold. But no, this was neither Edwin nor Harold. It was the ageless prowling thing out of the nightmare, the folk tale, the myth; it was what had terrified mankind since the human race had first learned to recognize the horror of primeval darkness—the horror that you pray above all things you may never have to meet in your waking hours.

And suddenly she could go no further: the stairway ended at a smooth leather door. She felt desperately on either side for a knob or a latch, but there was nothing to take hold of, and now the steps behind her were entering this last dark flight.

She leaned helplessly against the door and it swung back under her weight. She had to catch herself so as not to fall, and then looking about her found that she was in an enormous room. Moonlight streamed through high blank windows on to what looked like rows of coffins supported on little frames. It was the dissecting room that Dave had told her of, that covered most of the top floor, and out of which, by a winding stair you could climb to his office in the turret. She thought she remembered that the stairway was in one of the corners, but there was no way of telling which one. She moved swiftly to the right, past a series of glass cases in which she vaguely made out the white gleam of bones. There was no door, no stairway in this corner, and as she turned away the leather door swung open again, and Harold, the thing that was not Harold, stepped through.

She was standing in shadow just beyond the rim of one of the large windows through which she could see, over steep slopes of moonlit slate, a scattering of glittering water. For a flash she recalled her view of this same building, glowing rose-colored against the blue sky, as she had seen it this afternoon, from the canoe. If she passed these windows, her silhouette would stand out sharply. She must

157

crouch, and thus make her way unseen beneath the windows, to the next corner.

Bent almost double, she moved slowly along the wall. She could hear no sound; she could imagine that perhaps he had stepped silently over to this side of the room and was watching her from behind one of these tanks, but she did not dare to look up. Her back ached; her temples throbbed; but she reached the corner at last, and here was the stairway, winding upwards through a narrow pitch-black cylinder. Still crouching she put her foot on the first step. In a few steps she was completely out of sight. There could not be many more. The door at the top was locked. There was no light through any crack.

"Dave!" she whispered as loud as she dared. "Dave!"

No one answered. She leaned against the curving wall. She had known from the first, she had always known in her dreams, that it would be no use.

But she could not wait here, in this narrow trap. This of course would be where Harold would expect her to come; he would not know that she had found it by chance. She felt her way down the twisting stairs as quickly as she could without stumbling, and peered into the big moonlit room.

Harold stood not twenty feet away from her, between two rows of tanks. He was in full moonlight which gleamed on the blade in his hand. His eyes were holes of shadow but she felt that they were fixed on her.

"This explains why you were always so light in my dream," he said. "I did not even have to carry you, which is much better, because it would have been hard not to leave a trail."

Then before she knew it she had screamed, and as she ran between the tanks, in and out of the moonlight, she kept screaming and screaming until she lost even the echo of her own voice in a sickening swirl of blackness.

She was propped up in bed, in her own room once more. Terry had just left, and Dave was sitting beside her holding her hand. A fresh breeze from the lake floated in through the hickory leaves.

How did you know?"

"Paul deserves the credit," he said. "I haven't much to boast about. He had begun to suspect that Harold was growing unbalanced when Harold called on him, it must have been a couple of weeks ago, when he was so taken up with his sleuthing. He was rejected by the draft last year, you know, for psychological reasons. Then yesterday when he called Wanda, it struck Paul as queer enough for him to go and see him, and when he found him in his room he was convinced that something was wrong. Of course he didn't dream it would be as bad as it turned out. He wanted to warn you, though, and when you didn't telephone he began to worry, and they talked it over on the picnic and decided it was worth coming home to investigate. That was Jeanne's idea, and I'll be grateful to her as long as I live."

He pressed her hand. "Shall I go on?" he asked gently, "or are you too tired?"

She realized that she had closed her eyes. She opened them once more and smiled at him.

"Yes, do go on," she said. "I want to hear."

"Well, they stopped at my room, and luckily I was there, happy as a king and just going over the day in my mind. We separated and made the rounds of the various restaurants in town; though by that time we thought you'd probably be through. It occurred to me at last to call the Chicken Shack, and from my description they were sure you had been there. They said you had just left. That was fine; so I went back to my rooms where Paul and Terry were to meet me, and when we thought we would wait around your apartment. When you didn't turn up, we went to Harold's; and then just by the grace of God I happened to think of Harold's office. And there was a light, sure enough. I told Terry and Paul it was okay, and let myself in. Then it struck me that if you and he were having a perfectly innocent private conversation, if you were breaking your engagement, for example, you wouldn't be any too pleased to find me hanging around outside the door; so I sort of lingered for a bit in the lower hall, and then I thought I'd go a little further. I walked upstairs past Harold's office

159

really scared. It was just about then I thought I heard screams way up above, so faint I couldn't be quite sure, but from then on I really hustled."

"And Dave," she said with a faint shudder, "did you have a hard time with Harold?"

"Luckily I didn't have to tackle him alone. He ran out the main door when I pushed through the little swing door from the back stairs, and we found him later in his own room, Paul and I and a good husky policeman we'd brought with us. He didn't collapse like Edwin; he fought like the very devil. What scared him seemed to be the thought of going to Brookfield. He kept shouting that Edwin was expecting him but he wouldn't go. He was in such a panic at the idea I'm surprised he didn't use his own knife on himself before we got him. Paul gives a queer explanation—very queer, it seems to me, under the circumstances. He thinks that Harold was one of those people that can't bear the sight of their own blood. He must have known he'd be caught, but I think his mind was a bit confused. It must have been, or he wouldn't have gone straight home."

Daphne closed her eyes again. She was very tired, and the breeze from the lake made her think of the cool autumn days that would be coming soon.

"Speaking of home," Dave said, "I've already begun this morning looking for apartments. My present deferment is up November first. I'm not going to try to renew it, but that will give us a little over two months."

She felt suddenly too tired to answer, or even to lift her eyelids; but she pressed his fingers, and realized before she drifted off to sleep that this time she felt no impulse to delay her marriage.

THE END